The Water is Wide

Natalie Banks

Champion Books Publishing Company

Printed in the United States of America
The Library of Congress has cataloged this edition as follows:
The Water is Wide/Natalie Banks
ISBN: 978-069-296-9892
(paperback/e-book)

Books by Natalie Banks

- The Water is Wide
- The Dark Room coming early 2018. (See the last page of this book for a preview.)

Follow her on

Twitter: Natalie_Banks_
Facebook page: Natalie Banks
Instagram: NatalieBanksNovels

*Go to **NatalieBanks.net** to sign up for her VIP list to receive exclusive information on upcoming books and early bird discounts.*

Acknowledgements

This book would have never been possible without the support of many extraordinary people. I owe so much to all of you.

I am so thankful to my family who stood by me during the long hours of writing, re-writing, and editing. Their support, love, and encouragement is priceless to me. Thank you to my wonderful husband Joe and my children Jesseca, Jake, Caroline, Ethan, Elisabeth-Grace. My little pods, Violet and Sawyer, you are lights that shine brightly in my life. And I cannot forget Truman and Finn. I love you all. Without you, I wouldn't be me.

I also want to thank the very special people who helped me see my manuscript from many different perspectives that I wouldn't have been able to see otherwise. They also gave me the encouragement and support I needed to believe in myself and this book. Bettina Atell, Ivy Martin, Rachael Hevrin, Amy Kurzeja, Brenda Stidham, and Donna Evans. Nancy Phillips, you made me accountable and didn't let me slide, you helped make this book what it is. You are all precious to me. Thank you for all the time you invested into me, and The Water is Wide.

I have to thank my wonderful first run editor Jim Banks. Who also happens to be the best father a girl could ever hope to have. Thank you for bringing a lifetime of editing experience to the table and not being afraid to tell me what you thought. This book would not exist without you.

I want to give a special thank you to my High School Creative Writing teacher, Emma Richardson. Thank you for inspiring me and helping me to believe in myself and my writing. I have never forgotten you.

I want to give a special thank you to Martijn Atell, Founder and CEO of VoteBash. His passion and drive inspire me every day! Thank you for all your encouragement and support. Check out his website at VoteBash.com!

Thank you to the people at Champion Books that helped bring this book into reality.

Last but not least I want to thank you, my readers. You are the ones who give fire to my soul and inspire me to go on. I not only write for myself, but I write for you.

Chapter 1

⸺⟨⬩⟩⸺

The day I came back to life, the sun shone just as brightly, as it did the day I died. It was supposed to be an ordinary day, and I was prepared for it. That's how I liked it. Each day the same as the one before it. Lifeless. Walking down the street, taking breaths, in and out, just like a living woman. It's funny how you can be living and dead, both at the same time. I had lived inside this deadness for so long now, I no longer remembered what it felt like to really be alive. I passed by people, blissful and full of ignorance, not seeing the truth of me, the walking dead, as my heels clicked loudly against the sidewalk. I fussed with my scarf repeatedly, as the wind kept blowing it directly over my eyes, forcibly blinding me. Over and over, like it was trying to keep me from seeing something ahead. If only I had listened.

I stopped, mid-step, nearly falling forward. I couldn't think, couldn't feel. Was I still breathing? I reached up to my chest to check and gasped at what was before me. My mind whirled out of control. No, it just couldn't be. It was impossible. Impossible! Time swirled in my mind. What day was it, what year? And then suddenly the blackness came. Clear, cool black relief.

1

People were talking all around me. I could hear their voices, but I couldn't make out what they were saying. Slowly, it started to tune in.

"Is she breathing?"

"Someone call 911!!!"

What was happening to me? I opened my eyes and was looking straight into the eyes that I had loved my whole life. He was looking right back at me, but the words.... the words.... They didn't make sense. Nothing made sense.

"Ma'am, are you okay? Can you hear me, ma'am?"

I sat up but then laid right back down.

He leaned over me and said, "Take your time, you took quite a fall."

The fall was the least of my worries at this point. My mind was spinning out of control, and all I knew was that I had to get out of there ....and fast.

People were staring, a lot of people. Usually, I would be embarrassed, but right now I couldn't collect a clear thought. It took a minute to get my bearings. Downtown Wilmington, noon, meeting Betsey for lunch. But not now, not anymore, I just needed to find my car. My head was throbbing, and I wobbled as I walked. People kept offering their assistance, to call for an ambulance, even a glass of water. I was trying to be polite, but I just wanted to leave. That was the only thing that could make this better right now. Clearing myself of the crowd proved to be more than difficult. Apparently, fainting makes you quite the celebrity. Under normal circumstances, Betsey and I would have found this funny. I was now a local celebrity. The lady who fainted in town square.

Though it only happened moments ago, I had already begun to doubt what I saw. He was similar. Very similar. And oh, those eyes. The eyes that penetrated my soul for 24 years, but it couldn't

2

be! Thomas had been dead for a long time. 14 years of loneliness had finally made me delusional.

Wandering, almost aimlessly, I steered myself away from the crowd. As if a sign from God, I suddenly spotted my little white Volvo. I welcomed the sight of something familiar. Something safe and certain. I drove home as fast as I possibly could, and once I pulled into the driveway, I realized I didn't even remember driving back.

Wilmington, North Carolina was our dream. A quaint southern city, situated right on the coast. And it was gorgeous in the Spring. This Spring was no different. I sat in the driveway, staring at the home we were supposed to live in together. We had purchased it right before he died. A two-story craftsman style, four-bedroom house. It had tan siding with black shutters and a cute little front porch. It was nestled in a quiet neighborhood right off of Oleander Drive. I loved the neighborhood, with the mature trees and sidewalks. The house had a beautiful pool and a place for me to plant a flower garden. It was the perfect house for our little family of four.

We stood outside in the front yard the day we came to see it, and he took me in his arms and kissed me right in front of the listing agent, and said: "Welcome home, beautiful!" At that moment, all negotiating power we had was gone. We had been toying with the idea of moving back to North Carolina for a while, and even though we hadn't sold our other home yet, he had insisted that we go ahead and buy this one. I was not keen on the idea. I wanted to be more practical. He kept assuring me that all would work out, and not to worry so much. Then he was gone. I had considered selling the Wilmington house right away, but in the end, our old house in Marblehead held too many painful memories for me to stay. There was pain in every fiber, every creaking floorboard, and around every corner. That was *our* home. We had christened each room when we bought it 21 years ago. Our first real home together. The place where we brought both our babies home from the hospital. We had so many happy memories in that house. Birthdays, Christmases, even our day to day life was filled with so many happy memories. Once Thomas was gone, I couldn't stand being there without him, so I sold it, and moved to North Carolina.

I still couldn't call this house, *my* home, it was our home, even though he had never spent one night here. It will always be mine and Thomas' home. Adam urged me to sell two years ago, to downsize, but I couldn't bear it. Selling this house would mean letting go of the final shreds of Thomas I had left.

I sat there in the driveway still shaking from the whole experience. It just wasn't real. It couldn't have been real. Well, I did faint, but the rest, not real...or was it? Right now, I couldn't trust my own mind.

I started out this morning like I do every morning for the last 14 years. Routine, it's what kept me going, what kept me sane.

I tried to remember, what exactly did I see?

I replayed the morning's events right up until I saw him. Running late, as always, I made my way down Market street with my scarf blinding me. Milling outside of The People's Bank was a group of people talking with great intensity. I was slightly intrigued to overhear what they were saying, but I was already running late. As I got ready to pass by the crowd, there he was, he stepped right out of the past and was there standing in front of me. But how could it have been him? I mean, Thomas had been dead for 14 years! How could I even begin to believe that I actually saw him? But I did believe it. I'd know those eyes anywhere. And suddenly I had the realization that my long dead heart was beating again.

Chapter 2

2002

The loudspeaker crackled a bit, as the pilot delivered the good news. "We are now making our descent, please fasten your seatbelts and remain seated." Cancun! Oh, how we had been awaiting this trip. Just the two of us, alone at last. The boys were with my neighbor, and I was sitting here with the man of my dreams, my husband, Thomas. Everyone always said how lucky we were to still be so in love after all these years. I didn't know if it was luck or not; I just knew he and I belonged together, and that's the way it would always be.

"The weather is 78 and sunny, hope you enjoy your stay in sunny Cancun." crackled the speaker again.

The plane skidded on the runway and slowly came to a stop at the gate. I looked over at Thomas, and he seemed a million miles away.

"Hey there handsome, it's time to get this party started," I giggled and moved past him in his seat.

I stopped suddenly in the aisle. My heart began to race. I had a terrible feeling come over me, a feeling of dread. I looked back at Thomas for reassurance; he was gathering our bags from the overhead compartment. I smiled. Everything was fine, everything was great actually, I shook it off, and we made our way off the plane.

The taxi cab rolled to a stop in front of The Grand Sol Resort, and it was just as magnificent as the brochures had proclaimed it would be. The main building had a red Spanish tiled roof, and peach colored stucco sides. Palm trees swayed in the wind. Flower nectar and salt spray perfumed the air. The property was gorgeous and seemed to go on for miles. Five glorious days and nights! We walked inside to the lobby. It was nothing less than spectacular. There was a large fountain running in the center that stood twice my height. There were huge potted palms in terracotta pots all around. Tropical green and yellow birds were flying around and landing in the pots. A Mariachi Band was playing. They were wearing huge sombreros and smiling ear to ear. We stood in line at the reception desk, and I snuggled up against Thomas. I felt like a newlywed again. We checked in, and the bellhop came over and put our luggage on a cart. He took us to our room immediately, even though check-in was not for another 2 hours. We had booked a deluxe cabana suite with its own private beach and pool. My expectations were high, and I was not disappointed! I gasped when we walked inside. The room was completely perfect. Just as I had imagined. Huge King size bed with a canopy and fluffy white bedding. And it had sheer fabric draped around it from floor to ceiling. There was a sitting area with a small sofa and table. On the table was a large vase filled with fresh orange and yellow flowers. I walked into the bathroom and was immediately in awe. It was so large; I could imagine a small family being able to live inside the space. It had orange clay tiled floors and walls. The shower was gigantic, with an overhead rain shower head. It had jets along its only wall, with the rest of the shower open to the bathroom. The sink was a vibrant blue hand painted pottery bowl, with tiny yellow flowers painted all over it. I was in love with this place already. And the view, the view. It was to die for. A wall of four large sliding doors that opened all the way up to give way to a perfect little beach, palm trees, a jacuzzi, and our own private pool.

"Thomas, can you even believe this place? I am in absolute heaven."

My words came back to me as if they had not even been spoken. I looked around and saw Thomas standing at the open wall, staring out at the ocean, lost in thought. I ran up behind him and put my arms around his waist. His body, just as strong and fit, as the day we met. He turned to me and smiled. We are so lucky, I thought, we really are. I breathed in his smell and sighed.

We spent most of our days lazing around the pool, swimming in the ocean, making love like newlyweds. I was in a dreamlike state the entire time. I could not believe tomorrow was our last day here; I actually felt a little resentful. I wasn't ready to go back. But I did miss the boys terribly, and besides, reality was pretty good for us. Better than most.

My best friend Betsey just found out her husband of 14 years was having an affair with his secretary. "How perfectly predictable!" she had said to me the last time I saw her. And then she cried, real tears. And Betsey never cried. My heart was breaking for her. I couldn't help but feel a little guilty for having it so good with Thomas. He was so good to me, good to our family. We had a really great life. A perfect life. And we certainly had made the most of this vacation. We took advantage of every moment together. We snorkeled twice, went on a sunset cruise, had dinner in the restaurant every night, drinking wine and talking for hours. I loved having Thomas all to myself. It was like we were college sweethearts all over again. We truly loved each other's company. We were not like most of our friends from college, who had married their college boyfriends or girlfriends. Most of them were divorced already, or could barely stand each other. And here Thomas and I were, still so desperately in love.

Since it was our last night, I pulled out the dress I had been saving. Something Thomas had never seen before. It was a black spaghetti strap chemise dress, with a super low V cut neckline. I opted to go bra-less. The material was thin and hung on my body just right. Sexy. Something I didn't always portray in our daily life. Mom clothes were the norm. But not tonight. I pulled my long blonde hair up into a loose bun, slipped on my stilettos, and made my grand entrance. I knew my effort had paid off by the look on Thomas' face. "Wow... just wow, honey..." His jaw dropped, and he just stared at me. I saw that spark in his eyes; it was still there.

He came up and started kissing my neck. "Can we skip dinner?"

I giggled but pulled away. "Not on our last night!"

I walked toward the door, "But, I promise I will make it up to you when we get back!" And I gave him a quick wink.

Thomas followed on my heels, "I'll take you up on that!" he laughed and swatted my butt as we walked out the door. I squealed with delight, as he pulled the door to.

Just before dawn, I saw Thomas' shadow move across the room.

"Are you okay?" I asked in a groggy voice.

His voice was strong and alert. I wondered how long he had been awake.

"Sure I am, I'm just going to go down to the beach, watch the sunrise, and maybe go for one last swim. Care to join me?"

I stretched and considered it for half a second. "No, go on without me, I'm going to rest here for a bit more before we have to leave."

He came over to the bed, "I figured my sleepyhead wouldn't go, but I'll miss you!"

He leaned in and kissed my lips, long and sweet. "I love you, Sarah, I hope you know that."

I whispered. "I love you too." But I wasn't sure if he had even heard me.

I rolled over and pulled the covers over my head, the taste of his lips still on mine and the smell of him surrounding me. I sighed and slipped back into dreamland.

Chapter 3

$\mathcal{I}$ paced back and forth across my Spanish tiled kitchen floor trying to digest what I saw. I was in shock. "Ridiculous!" shouting out to no one. I was crying and then a moment later was laughing at how foolish I was being. I was really starting to believe that maybe I was delusional. How could I even believe for one moment that it was Thomas? Him being there was impossible, I had to be crazy to believe it. There was no other explanation. It would not be the first time that my mental stability had come into question. I knew everyone had grave concerns for my wellbeing after Thomas died. I was consumed with guilt and grief. I withdrew from everything and everyone that I loved. Life didn't make sense anymore, and, why would it? All my dreams were planned around "us", and there was no longer an us. It took years for me to begin to live a shell of a life. I put on a good show though. For the boys. They needed me. Adam was 8 and Blake was only 5 when Thomas died. Both boys were blonde like me. But Adam had his father's eyes, piercing blue eyes, that could see straight through you. Their little tan bodies splashing and swimming in the pool reminded me to keep breathing. But nothing could resuscitate my dead heart. I was just as gone as Thomas. But for some awful reason, my body was still here. Left here, to survive without him. And I was partly to blame.

I didn't make any attempts to be a functioning person for the first six months after I lost Thomas. I retreated inside myself. I stayed in pajamas a good portion of most days; and most of those days, I stayed in my bed. I hired a nanny to come and help me care for the boys. I was lucky if I stepped outside of the house two days a month. I turned off service to my phone. The school had the nanny's number if the boys needed anything. I could not deal with one more well-meaning phone call. Even Betsey, my BFF, my female soulmate, was semi-ostracized from my life. I felt like the living dead. A zombie, defying the laws of science. I felt invisible. Lost. Alone. It was like I was screaming and screaming, and no one, not one single person could hear me. Somehow, I made it through, each day, sunrise to sunset. I did not care about anyone, or anything, except my boys. My body kept moving, only for them. It was after that six months of hell; I decided I had to make some real changes in order to survive this. That is when we made the move to Wilmington. I thought a new city would give me hope. In reality, I just learned how to pretend better.

Both boys were in college now. Adam was attending the University of North Carolina at Wilmington, because it was close, and he refused to be more than 20 minutes away from me. He took on the role of caretaker right from the beginning. He had always been there for me. Tender hearted boy. He sat with me for hours when I cried myself to sleep at night. He would hear me crying from his bedroom, and creep into my room in his cookie monster slippers, all fuzzy and blue, and crawl up next to me. His small hand patting my arm softly. He never said a word. He would just sit there with me until I fell asleep. Some mornings he would still be there, curled up in a little ball, fast asleep. Other mornings I would see him back in his own little bed with his Ninja Turtles bedspread tucked in under his chin. He was such a sweet boy. I know he missed Thomas almost as much as I did. Thomas was the one who taught him to hit a baseball, and when he made the team, Thomas never missed a game. Oh, how I wished Thomas could see him now. He would be so proud. Adam, always the overachiever, graduated with his Bachelor's degree at the top of his class, just last year. Now he was working on getting his masters in Psychology, his eyes set on a Ph.D. I couldn't help but wonder if it was my mental decline after Thomas' death, that spurred his interest in the subject. Should I feel guilty or be proud? I wasn't sure.

Blake, on the other hand, he took after his mother. He withdrew. He went from an always giggling child to a sullen and moody boy. I think somehow, he blamed me. Thomas and I left together, and I came back alone. In his 5-year-old little mind, he could not comprehend how that happened. I don't think he ever forgave me. I know I haven't forgiven myself, so how could I expect him to? If only I had gotten up that morning, and gone with Thomas to watch the sunrise, and to swim. Why God didn't I?

Blake played and acted like a normal little boy most days, but I saw the change in him. And the emptiness in his eyes. I wondered if anyone saw that in mine too? He was so clingy to Thomas. He was always from day one, a daddy's boy. When we brought him home from the hospital, Thomas was the only one who could get him to stop crying. His first word was Da-da, and his first step was right into his daddy's arms. He adored Thomas, and life without him, took the floor out from under his small little world.

Blake left for college two years ago. He chose to go to school in California. Berkley. As far away from me as possible. He was majoring in business, just like Thomas. We hadn't seen him since 2 Christmases ago. He didn't come home last year. He had a girlfriend out there now, and he had spent the holidays with her family. She was a native California girl. Pretty brunette. He met her on the beach one day by chance, and after that they were inseparable. Sometimes I felt a little jealous, because he never let me in, the way he let her in. He shut me out completely. He was still close with Adam, however. He and Adam spoke on the phone weekly and texted daily. Adam kept me apprised of what was going on. He always made excuses to me, about why I didn't hear from Blake. But I knew the truth. I know Adam feels bad about the relationship between his brother and me, but there was nothing, that even he, could do to fix it. That ship had sailed many years ago. Adam, on the other hand, did not have a steady girl. He never had a relationship that lasted more than 2-3 weeks. I think, actually I know, it is more to do with me, than with his choices in women. I think he feels, if he gave any of himself away, that he would neglect me. He's the one who's here for me, mowing the grass, making repairs, hanging pictures, taking Thomas' place. On top of keeping up a 4.0 grade average and working his part-time job at the local Social Services office. He had his hands full. I feel guilty about him spending so much time here, but I'm so thankful too. I have told him numerous times to not worry so much about me. I was getting stronger each day. Plus, I wanted to be a little more independent. And if need be, there were plenty of handymen and landscapers to do things for me. But he still insisted. Secretly I was glad to have him here so often. I did get lonely sometimes. He did not want me spending money on things that he could do for me. But I had the money to hire help. Boy, did I have the money. Between the life insurance policy that Thomas had coincidentally upped the coverage on right before the trip, and the "please keep this quiet" money

13

from the resort, I had a pretty hefty bank account. I didn't have many expenses once I paid off the two houses and cleared Thomas' debts from his business. And those debts actually turned out to be quite a bit of money. Thank God, I had the insurance money to pay it. I could have lost both the houses and anything else that wasn't bolted down. After all of that was done, I still had a good amount of money to take care of the boys, send them to college, and live a very comfortable life. Though those weeks prior to getting that insurance check were a living hell for me. The insurance company was uncooperative right from the very beginning. They gave me such a hard time. Some men had even shown up in Mexico and started questioning me about Thomas' death. Then they had an agent following me and questioning me for weeks after I came home. After the authorities issued a death certificate for Thomas, the Insurance agency backed off. But occasionally, I still would see someone watching me, for months afterward. It seemed as if they had as hard a time accepting Thomas' death, as I did.

My boys gave me purpose and Wilmington gave me a place to live, where I didn't see Thomas around every corner. Eventually, I began functioning in the real world. I took the boys to Scouts, tennis lessons, and baseball practice. I smiled. I laughed. I talked to people like I was completely fine. I did my best to try to build a life. But that ache, the longing for Thomas, it never left me. The pain never dulled. In the beginning, it was expected for me to be in despair, but after a few months, no one felt sorry for me anymore. They all expected me to move on. But I couldn't get past it. I did make attempts to move on, but part of me was gone forever. And I didn't know how to recollect myself. I could only start over. Find a new version of me to be.

As I paced around the kitchen, I suddenly realized the time. 2:00 pm. My heart jumped. How had I lost all that time? Adam was coming over any minute to do the lawn. His classes were over at 1:30 pm, and he usually came straight here. I couldn't let him know what I saw. I mean, what I thought I saw. Good Lord, he will have me committed. All he had to do was take one look at my face, and he would know something was wrong. I grabbed my purse and keys, scribbled a note for Adam about running errands, and I was out the door. But as the door slammed shut, the note slipped right off and slid under the entrance table.

Chapter 4

I drove along Highway 74 in silence. It didn't even occur to me to turn the radio on. I drove on with determination, like I was actually going somewhere, but where, I didn't know. I just had to go. Seeing Adam right now would've been a terrible mistake. Whatever happened to me today, whatever it was I saw, who I saw, no one, especially me, was ready to handle it. So, I drove.

I drove, seeing nothing but the pavement and Thomas' face in front of me. I got on the interstate, and before I knew it, I found myself exiting, heading toward Selma. The place where Thomas and I met. What was I doing here? Did I think the answers were hidden somehow in the place where it all started?

It was 4 o'clock by the time I hit Pollock street. It seemed as if no time had passed at all. The little rural town was just as quiet as it was nearly 24 years ago. My god, had it really been that long? I sighed, feeling all of my 44 years weighing on me. I looked in the rearview mirror at myself. My once long blonde hair was tinseled with gray and cut into a perfect little bob. "It's all the rage," my stylist told me, as she cut 14 inches off. My green eyes looked tired, accented by the lines that had made themselves at home around them. I always had a fresh, girl next door look, people told me. But I certainly wasn't looking so fresh anymore. Some people may still consider me beautiful, but I didn't see myself that way anymore.

The town seemed untouched by time. I drove along East Railroad street and over the railroad tracks. I drove past Rick's General Store with its handmade rockers outside and red potted flowers all around the porch. They still had a large American flag flying off one of the porch columns. I remembered thinking it was charming the way they made it seem so homey. I drove on down the street a little way and came to a stop right in front of Then Again Antique Shop. The place where my life was forever changed. I stared, trying to get a glimpse of the inside, and suddenly became aware there was honking. A blue Chevy Nova with a cracked windshield was behind me, and the driver was ticked. "Move on lady!" a distinguished looking gentleman yelled out to me. And by distinguished gentleman, I mean, a grease covered, overall wearing, long-haired, madman. I stepped on the gas and floored it out of there. I looped around the block and stopped on a side street. A few kids were walking around in a group and staring down at their phones. Socializing, the modern way. I locked my car doors. I didn't know if my new gentleman friend held grudges or not. I sat there one block over from the very place where I first laid eyes on Thomas' handsome face, and I started to cry. Why was this happening to me? I had finally reached a place in my life where I was okay. I had my weekly lunch with Betsey, my art class, my flower garden, and I was even considering volunteering at the art museum once a week. I was building some sort of a life for myself. My grief, though still there, was starting to take a back seat, rather than a dominating factor in everything I did. I would never be the old me again, but I was learning a lot about the new me.

And now suddenly, Thomas was back from the dead, or his doppelganger had somehow cruelly found me, and crossed my path. Whatever the case, my life was turned upside down, and there was no way to turn it right side up again. All those horrible old feelings were back. All the hurt and loss pumped through my veins again, just as sharply as it did 14 years ago. But this time things were a little different, this time I actually had hope.

***

My mind drifted back in time to 1994. I was 19 years old and the editor of my college newspaper. I had been attending the University of North Carolina at Chapel Hill for three years. I graduated a year early from high school at the age of 16 and got a head start on my college education. "Gifted" is what they called me. High expectations, is what I heard.

Growing up in a family of doctors and lawyers, I had never wanted for anything. My parents were lawyers, my mom's parents were doctors, and my dad's parents were lawyers. My two brothers, James and David, were lawyers too. A family tradition had been started. I was the surprise baby, coming when my brothers were 14 and 16. I was the quintessential spoiled little girl. I had everything I could ever have dreamed of, while growing up. We lived in Boston in a huge white mansion on North Main street. Well known among Bostonians as the elite place to live. I attended Carlston Academy, one of the best primary schools in the nation. I had a horse that was kept at Cameron Equestrian Center a few miles away, with riding lessons weekly. I ate lunch at the Country Club with my parents and both sets of Grandparents every Sunday. Needless to say, they expected a lot from their little "golden girl", which was, in fact, my nickname growing up because of my golden blonde hair. "Where is my little golden girl?" my Grandfather James would exclaim every time he came into our house. "That's my little golden girl," my Grandmother Lily would say when she squeezed me close against her large engineered breasts. Even my parents called me Golden Girl. I didn't hate the nickname, but I certainly didn't love it. And I was definitely mortified when Laura Turner heard it. Needless to say, it went around school pretty quickly. But as most things do with kids, the allure of teasing me wore off, and it stopped. But I still begged my family never to call me that again. And they didn't. Instead, they called me Gigi. Short for Golden Girl. When I chose to go to school in North Carolina instead of Harvard and chose Journalism as my major instead of law or medicine, the Golden Girl started to lose her shine. And when I brought home sweet Thomas to meet them, there wasn't even a shimmer left. They certainly did not approve of Thomas, my choices, or me any longer.

The first time I saw Thomas, it was a rainy Thursday. I had gone to Selma, NC to get a story for the paper. It was a small school paper, but I treated my job as if I worked for the New York Times. I loved Journalism. Telling the stories of life. Bringing the world to print. It brought me to life.

I had heard that Selma celebrated a festival called Railroad Days and I had drove down from Chapel Hill, in the rain, to get the story first-hand. It was only an hour and 5 minutes from school, and I had the time to spare.

By the time I had arrived, the rain had stopped, and the sun was out. I didn't have a lot of competition to scoop this story. There were a few other reporters there from the local papers nearby, but no major networks were out here trying to cover this small festival. I was excited nonetheless. The locals were out in droves. I never quite understood southerners, but I quite liked them. They were so much nicer than the people I grew up around. They had a way of making you feel comfortable and like family, even if you had only known them 5 minutes. Southern charm is what they called it.

I spent the day taking photos of the Railroad Days Beauty Queen contestants, Caboose runners, Food tables, model train displays, and groups playing gospel and bluegrass music. There was booth after booth of delicious baked desserts and homemade crafts. Little hand sewed dolls, crocheted hot pads, wood carvings, and hand painted artwork. Not like any art I had seen in the galleries in Boston, but definitely charming. There was even a booth with free puppies. I must have spent twenty minutes, loving on those puppies and getting free puppy dog kisses. There were fried foods for sale everywhere. Fried cakes, fried pickles, fried fish, fried steak. The aromas were all around, making my tummy growl, but I wasn't quite ready to take the leap to fried foods. The only fried food I had ever eaten before was French fries. Everyone was smiling and laughing. Not a sour face in sight. I even got to take a picture of the mayor for my story. It was quite an event. For October, it was still pretty hot and humid. I had not yet adjusted to this Southern weather. I walked around looking for a place to sit down in the shade. Finally, I found a spot under a big Maple tree. I spent a while watching the festival attendants. Men in cowboy hats and boots. Little girls in southern ball gowns. Baseball hats and Wrangler jeans. A lot of hugging and exclamations of "Hey Y'all." Foreign but lovely, all the same. I noticed the time, it was after lunch already, and I had a class at 3. I got up and headed to my car; I would make it in plenty of time.

As I drove down Pollock road, I started to feel queasy, in fact, I felt like I might black out. I turned down Railroad street and parked as quickly as I could, jumped out and ran into the closest place I could see, and that was the Then Again Antique Store. I needed something to drink and fast. The lady behind the counter, with her sweet Southern drawl, said, "Can I help you darlin'?" And before I could speak, I was down on the floor. Everything was fuzzy, and my head hurt. I closed my eyes and winced.

I opened my eyes, and the sweetest southern lady with dark curls and chubby round cheeks was fanning my face. "Oh darlin', I do believe you have done and gotten yourself overheated! You want me to getcha somethin' to drink?"

I managed to nod yes. She blared out to a young boy in a white t-shirt and jeans standing nearby "Don't just stand there, get her here a drink, and make it fast!"

He came back with an ice-cold bottle of soda, a glass bottle, no less.

"Here you go darlin'; this will fix ya right up."

I sat up and took a few sips. It, in fact, did make me feel better. Surprising how a chemically sweetened liquid could do so much good, and apparently it was exactly what I needed. I hadn't had a sip of water or a bite to eat all day. The heat and lack of food had gotten the best of me. Her face was very close to mine. "You need yourself a BC Powder, that's powerful medicine." She was nodding her head in encouragement.

"Oh, no thank you. You are so kind though." I spoke softly to her, wondering what exactly a BC Powder was.

"Well don't ya worry a lick about it, you just rest here until you feel more like yourself again. My name is Darla; you just call out if you need somethin'." She headed back to her counter in her bedazzled Levi's and hot pink high heels with dark curls bouncing. She was adorable.

I sat gathering my bearings. I was so glad I had stopped here when I did. I looked around; this was apparently a novelty shop of sorts, antiques, I was pretty sure. Just the kind of place that I could get lost in for hours. I wish I had the time to stay and look around.

She had old tools, musical instruments and antique metal advertisements hanging on the walls that advertised cigars, sodas, and soap; all at the low cost of 1 cent! There were toys and dishes that were loved and used many years ago. Lots of antique and vintage furniture too. Some antique tools were on display. An old saw and spinning wheel sat in a corner forgotten by time. The store smelled of old books and dust; I liked that smell. It makes you feel as if you were trespassing in a time or place where you didn't belong. A sneak peek of the past. Inside the counter on which the register stood, were old cameras, jewelry, watches, and a few LP records that I could see. Near where I was sitting was an old wooden trunk. I couldn't help but wonder what treasures of the past it had held. Just then the store door chimed, and in walked two young guys. Cute, really cute, both of them. One had strawberry blonde hair and the other dark brown hair, both with strong athletic builds. I was at once acutely aware that I was sitting on the dusty store floor against the wall, like one of the forgotten items of the past. I wished at that moment that I had attempted to make myself up a little bit today. I had not put much thought into what I was wearing. I had thrown on a Ralph Lauren t-shirt with jeans and threw my hair into a ponytail. Not exactly what you want to be wearing the first time you meet a cute guy. But, I was never one to go to the extreme with hair and makeup like most girls. I was always told that I was naturally pretty, and that's the road I took, the more natural approach, but at times like this, I wished I had the frills and sass to hide behind. They walked over to my sweet southern caretaker, and I overheard them ask her about baseball cards. She shook her head "Nope, we sure don't have any of them collectible sporting cards. I've never seen much use in them," the boys looked at each other and smiled. Then the red-haired boy said, "Thanks anyway ma'am," and they turned to walk out. At that moment, the dark haired one looked over straight in my direction. Oh god, he sees me, I thought. I wanted to disappear. Keep going, I silently willed him, keep going. But no, he did not obey, he turned and headed straight for me.

Chapter 5

2002

A stream of sunlight broke through the cracks of the thick white drapes that covered the doors and nudged me awake. I stretched and rolled over, looking for Thomas. Feeling around with my eyes still closed, he wasn't there. I opened my eyes. Empty pillow. Wait, what time was it? I reached for my phone. It took a moment for it to come into focus. I gasped, 8 am. Oh my God, our flight!

"Thomas!" I yelled as I was getting up. I grabbed my clothes and began to dress as quickly as possible. Our flight was in 45 minutes!

"Thomas, we are late!" I yelled toward the bathroom door.

He didn't answer. I ran over and banged on the closed door.

"Honey, are you in there?" No answer. Damnit! Where is he, and why did he let me sleep in? I was in too much of a hurry to be mad.

I ran around the room gathering our belongings as fast as I could, shoving everything I could grab into our bags. I got everything packed and got myself somewhat ready in 10 minutes.

Thomas still hadn't returned. I wondered if maybe he had fallen asleep on the lounge chairs outside watching the sunrise? I peeked out the window drapes, and the chairs were empty. I opened one of the doors to go out there to double check. No Thomas. The sun shone brightly down, causing me to squint. A seagull called out. I ran back inside.

It occurred to me that he's probably gone down to grab us coffees and muffins to go. I called down to the front desk and requested a hand with the bags. I would just find Thomas in the lobby, and we can catch a cab. We still had 35 minutes! We can make it. I looked around the room one last time. The room had a lived-in look. Pillows on the floor, unmade bed. Room Service dishes on the table from the midnight cheese fries and beer we had ordered last night. Just then I remembered my yellow beach towel was out by the pool. I ran outside and grabbed it, still damp, and shoved it into my carryon bag. My brain raced, was that everything? I hated to have to rush, but there was no other choice. I looked out at the ocean, and for a moment a cold shiver went down my spine, I didn't know why, but didn't have time to care.

The bellboy knocked just as I was opening the door. He took the bags, and we hurried down to the lobby together. I asked him to hail a cab for me and stay with the luggage while I went to get Thomas. I ran as fast as I could, with my bed head hair, looking around wildly. I had forgotten to brush it. I realized that I must look like a lunatic. I reached into my purse and tied the mess into a low ponytail. I kept going, looking for Thomas to appear. I rushed into the buffet area, still no Thomas. Bewildered, I checked the hotel gym and coffee bar. Nothing. I looked around racking my brain, thinking of where else he could be. I was getting angrier and more frustrated by the minute. I ran to the gift shop; maybe he was picking up something for the boys? But he wasn't there either.

Then it hit me. I realized that I probably just missed him. He was more than likely back at the room looking for me too. I walked back through the stream of people and waited by the front doors of the hotel. The breeze was gusting in, every time the large glass doors slid open and shut. Lots of people were checking out this morning too. Walking past me, dragging their bags behind them. All were looking sullen and disappointed that reality had called their name. This is where he will come looking for me once he realizes I have left the room with the bags. I'll be here when he comes down, and he will smile. And I know once I see his face, I won't be angry anymore. I could never be angry at Thomas for long. He had better hurry though; we were down to 25 minutes.

Chapter 6

1994

$\mathcal{I}$ felt my face burning with heat, embarrassment, or both, as the dark-haired boy came toward me. He smiled, and boy did he have the best smile. My heart began to pound.

He leaned over me. "Hi there, are you okay?"

I couldn't speak.

"I saw you sitting down here on the floor, and wanted to check on you."

I just sat there dumbfounded and just stared, his eyes were the most crystal blue I had ever seen. He looked like he had just stepped out of a movie scene, with his perfectly chiseled jawline, and muscular body and smooth tanned skin. I realized he had stopped talking and was just looking at me, waiting for an answer. Speak, Sarah, speak!

"Hi... yeah, I'm okay..."

I could feel my face burning even more with embarrassment.

"I just got a little overheated at the Railroad Days Festival, and stopped in here for a drink." I laughed and tried to sound nonchalant.

He smiled again. Oh my god, that smile.

"Well, I'm sure glad you're okay. I'm Thomas by the way," He said as he reached out his hand to help me up.

"I'm Sarah; it's nice to meet you." I smiled as I dusted off my shorts.

We walked out of the store together. His redheaded friend was nowhere in sight. The sun was still high in the sky, but a breeze had picked up, and the heat was no longer oppressive.

"Do you live around here?" Thomas asked sheepishly.

"Actually, no, I am a journalist in school at UNC-Chapel Hill covering Railroad Days," I said with pride.

He laughed. "What? No way! I go to school at NC State. That's not too far from you at all!"

With his tone, I could tell that he liked me, despite me being underdressed for the occasion.

"So, where's your friend?" I asked, looking around.

"Stephen? Who cares, why don't *you* just give me a ride back?" he laughed flirtatiously.

"And anyway, this isn't the first time he's left me behind," he laughed again.

For a moment, I was a little scared. I didn't know this guy at all. What if he was a rapist or a murderer?! Then I looked into those crystal blue eyes again, and I was helpless to say no.

We drove back toward Raleigh talking and laughing comfortably, like two friends who had known each other forever. We got to Raleigh and drove down Gresham Blvd. I pulled into his apartment building parking lot and pulled into a parking space. And we just kept talking. It was 3:15. I had missed my class. But I didn't care. In fact, I was happy just sitting there listening to him talk and thinking dreamily to myself; I could do this for the rest of my life.

He had grown up in Shallotte, NC. A little coastal town. He told me of the struggles his single mother had raised him and his brother. His mother was never around though. She worked two jobs to keep up. His father had abandoned them when his little brother was born. Thomas had not seen him since. He and his brother practically raised themselves; they were only ten months apart, so they were more like twins. He told me of their adventures and mishaps down in the "blackwater, " and the many days they spent together on the beach. He told me how they had done everything together. His brother was his best friend. He teared up when telling me that his baby brother had been killed in car accident when he was only 15 years old. While joyriding in a friend's mom's car, they had run off of the road and hit a tree. His brother's name was Adam. His mother was never the same after that. She drank a lot, and Thomas was left alone in more ways than one. He worked nights and weekends at the local supermarket as a bag boy. Trying to make money to help his mom out. Her drinking had gotten so bad that she couldn't make the bills anymore. Then he found her one day, lying on the couch, with an empty liquor bottle on her chest. She fell asleep and never woke up again. He spent the rest of his senior year living with different friends, just trying to make it to graduation. He told me that going away to college was the only thing that saved him.

He was majoring in business at State. He was dedicated and hardworking. And an avid baseball fan. He told me of how he watched every single one of his high school's baseball games. His mother could never afford to let him play. He collected baseball cards too, hence the reason he was at the Antique Store in Selma. He was always on the lookout for old collectible cards. God, he was cute. And smart. I was smitten.

I told him of growing up in Boston, careful to leave out the wealthy and privileged part, and how much I loved riding horses growing up. I told him of my love for journalism. And I told him about my two protective older brothers. He joked that he was terrified of that news.

"I hope they don't come beat me up for high jacking their sister!"

We both laughed. He just kept looking at me and smiling. Sometimes so intently that it would make me blush.

"You know, you're the prettiest girl I've ever seen?" He said it with an intense sincerity in his eyes.

"Thank you, Thomas, you know you're not too bad yourself!" Laughing, I told him in return, but that was an understatement. We sat there in my car that day until well past 7. He offered to take me to get a meal, but I refused.

"I need to go," I told him.

Why I didn't know, but I was feeling completely overwhelmed with all of it. Something about him stirred something in me that I did not recognize. I had never felt anything like this before. I gave him my number and drove away happier than I had been in years.

I drove back to school, wondering if I would ever hear from him again or would he just be the star of my dream guy fantasies from this day forward. I didn't have a roommate or a pet. Just my furniture was waiting on me when I got home. As I walked in the door of my Garden studio apartment, my phone was ringing. I ran to grab it; my heart gripped with hope. I saw it was him on the caller ID and I squealed with delight. We talked until midnight, munching on snacks, and laughing at each other's stories. I hung up that night knowing that today was the first day of the rest of my life.

And it was. I graduated in 1994, and for my graduation present, he gave me an engagement ring. "I never want to be away from you," he said down on one knee.

I knelt down to face him, and tears were streaming down my face, "I never want to be away from you either."

He graduated that Spring too. We were married that fall, in Boston at Old North Church, with my parents, grandparents, and a thousand of their closest friends' disapproving looks.

I didn't care; I was the happiest girl in the world. And when Thomas lifted me up and carried me into our little one-bedroom apartment in North End, I knew I never wanted any more.

We moved to Boston to find jobs. Thomas wanted to move there to be close to my family. He was hoping it would rekindle some of the connections I had lost by marrying him, though it didn't help at all. There was nothing Thomas, nor I could do to win their approval now. Thomas got a job immediately at Benway & Fitch Investments. He started at the bottom, but he was happy. I got hired at The Beantown Chronicle doing wedding announcements, and I was happy too. We had each other, and that's all that really mattered. We had sex every night and talked until the wee hours of the morning. We were friends, as much as we were lovers. We went to Red Sox baseball games on the weekends, ate hot dogs and drank beer. We just loved being together. For the first time in my life, I didn't feel alone. I had nothing to prove. I wasn't the golden girl anymore, but the golden band around my finger more than made up for it.

Not long after that, Thomas started his own investment company with his best friend from college, Neil Stetson, and I got pregnant with Adam, his brother's namesake. I decided to quit working and stayed home with the baby. I loved being a mom and a wife. We bought a little blue cape cod style three-bedroom house in Marblehead, only 40 minutes from the city right before Adam was born. We loved that little house. Thomas worked so hard updating it and keeping it up. We were a happy little family. Then we got pregnant with Blake, and our family was complete.

When Thomas kissed me, my toes still tingled, my heart still raced, and my skin got warm. We were still in love. On summer nights, after the boys went to bed, we would lie outside on a blanket and gaze up at the stars.

"Life couldn't be any better than it is right at this moment," Thomas said one night as he stared up into the night sky. I scooted up next to him, and he put his arm around me.

"I couldn't agree more," I said in almost a whisper.

When Blake was 4, Thomas began to change. He was moodier, worked later than he used to, and I started to worry. Was he was having an affair? I tried to talk to him, but he would force a smile and tell me everything was fine.

He would say, "Sarah, stop worrying so much."

I tried to listen, but I couldn't shake the feeling that something wasn't right. He also worried a lot about how much money we were spending. I was never that good at budgeting, because I had never had to watch money before. I had asked my parents for money once, to help out, and Thomas was furious with me.

"I don't want a hand out from your stuck-up parents. They already think I'm worthless, Sarah!" His face said it all.

I felt so ashamed. After that, I didn't push him about the money or dare ask my parents for a dime again. I started learning how to budget. All I wanted was for Thomas to be happy. But his moodiness got worse, and I was getting very concerned. One day I even followed him. The only thing that I saw that was unusual was him meeting with some men in black suits at a café down the road from his office. Different than his usual in-office client meetings, but nothing else seemed to be out of the ordinary. I felt so foolish and guilty for not trusting him. But things did not get better. The late nights were more often than not. He even started neglecting the boys, and we hadn't had sex in 5 weeks. I felt like I was going to die. And he wouldn't talk to me. I kept asking him what was wrong, but I got nothing out of him. I started checking his pockets and smelling his clothes for women's perfume. I was becoming more despondent. Was it me? Maybe he wasn't happy with our life. I wished he would just talk to me.

Then one day out of the blue, he came home, and he was the old Thomas again. He was smiling and joking like he used to. I didn't know where the change came from, but I didn't care! I had my Thomas back. And that night when he took me into his arms and starting kissing my neck, I was completely happy again.

The next few months were wonderful. Thomas spent, even more, time at home than he had before. We had weekly date nights, and we were like two teenagers who couldn't keep their hands off each other. He spent a lot of time playing with the boys. We cooked out on the BBQ grill, and we were even talking about putting in a pool. We were lying in bed late one night, and he said: "Sarah, I'm really sorry I've been so distant lately." He was staring up at the ceiling.

"I was really stressed at work, but I got a new deal, and things are going really well now. I'm sorry that you suffered because of it." He still didn't look at me, only the ceiling.

I squeezed up next to him, "It's alright, I'm just glad you're okay, and I'm glad we're okay."

"I was actually afraid you were having an affair..." I said almost sheepishly.

Thomas looked over at me and laughed heartily, "You silly girl, you're the only one in this world for me, now and forever." He pulled me closer, and I forcibly put away the nagging doubt that something was still not quite right.

Chapter 7

*dam pulled up at his mom's house. No car in the driveway? "Where the heck is she?" he said to himself as he got out of the car. It wasn't like her to not be home in the afternoon. She was very stringent to a schedule. You could set a watch to it. He picked up his phone and dialed her number. No answer. He went to the storage building and got out the lawnmower. It took a few tries, but it started. This was the same mower that his dad had used. Still running strong. *I'm not sure if I'm still running strong*, he mused. The weight of graduate school and taking care of his mom 24/7, was beginning to wear thin on him. Especially now that he had met somebody. Somebody wonderful. He wanted, no he needed, to give more of his time to her. Her name was Emily. She was amazing. They'd met in the school library eight weeks ago. She was in her 3rd year, studying architecture. Not a usual field for a girl, but she was up for it. And she was beautiful; god was she beautiful. Long brown hair, freckles across her button nose, and her body, she was a goddess. All the right curves, in all the right places. And she made him laugh, the always so serious Adam, who didn't have time to laugh. At least that's what everyone said about him. But when he was with Emily, everything was different; he was different. Freer, more himself, than he had ever been. For the first time in Adam's life, he was uncertain of what to do. He had always been certain of everything. Even when his dad died, he knew what he had to do. Take care of mom. She was so sad and weak. And she didn't have anyone but him, and her friend Aunt Betsey. Betsey wasn't really his aunt, but she had been part of his life so long, that she had adopted the role. Not that there was a lack of suitors or friends for mom.

She was a beautiful woman, even in her 40's, she was still stunning. Men and women alike instantly liked her. But she was closed off to everyone and everything. She had numerous offers for dates but refused every single one. Always some excuse of why the guy wasn't right. She thinks she can fool me with this "I've got a life" business, but Adam knew better. She was always offering to have a handyman or landscaper come and take care of the house, but deep-down, Adam knew she really wanted it to be him. Dad dying had stripped his beautiful, vibrant mother of her life. She made a living being a grieving widow. But now there was Emily, and he desperately needed to take her up on the offer to bring in help.

Blake was of no use. Running off to school in California. Not bothering to come home last Christmas.

I pretended to understand, but I was actually pretty ticked. Girl or no girl, family comes first. He was just never able to forgive mom for coming back from Mexico without dad. Blake was just so little, and he didn't understand. It was strange though, dad's disappearance, but the police had cleared Mom, and no one could ever believe that she would hurt dad. She loved him more than life itself. But Blake, nonetheless, looked at her with disdain. And he never got past it. Even today, he pretends he's okay, but inside he's got so much anger. I've even tried to help him work past it, but when someone doesn't want to change, you can't make them.

Blake does call Mom on the very rare occasion, but its only surface conversation. I guess I'm lucky that he stays in touch with me at all. But honestly, I can't help but have a little bitterness. How could he just leave me to deal with all this responsibility? I really didn't mind that much before, but now there was Emily. How could I spread myself any thinner? I think I have given enough. And why can't Mom just buck up and move on now. It has been "poor Mom" for 14 years; enough is enough. Even without Emily, this gig was getting pretty old. I was going to have to talk to mom, and soon. The hours I was putting in at school, my job at the Social Services Office which I love, and now having time for Emily too, it was all too much for me to manage. I didn't want to give up any part of it, I can usually handle anything thrown at me, but now I was breaking down.

I went along with my thoughts and mowed the front yard and half of the back. Then stopped for a break and went inside for a drink. Poured myself some iced tea. Still no sign of mom. I picked up the phone and tried her again, no answer. This was starting to get a little eerie. I decided to finish the yard, and if she's still wasn't back by then, I was going to have to do something. It was six by the time I finished the mowing and weed trimming. Now, I was really starting to panic. I called Emily and told her I wouldn't be able to meet her for dinner tonight. I didn't tell her why she just took my word for it. I couldn't tell her about my mom, not the truth about how my mom really is. I was afraid it would scare her off. She's so solid, so grounded. A girl like that would not want to be burdened down with my family problems. I tried mom's phone again. This time it went straight to voicemail without ringing. Was her battery dead now? I wanted to drive around and look for her. But where would I go? I had no idea of where to start. Instead, I called Aunt Betsey.

Betsey answered on the first ring. Her sweet familiar voice saying "Hello" brought little comfort.

"Aunt Betsey, its Adam."

"Hi sweetie, what a pleasant surprise!"

"I wish it were a pleasant call, but I'm calling about Mom..."

Aunt Betsey immediately sounded panicked, "What do you mean, what's wrong? I've actually been a little worried about her myself because she didn't show up for our lunch date today."

I felt the blood drain from my body. "She didn't meet you today? Why didn't you call me?"

"Oh my gosh Adam, I didn't really think it was serious, this isn't the first time she's stood me up you know." She half laughed.

Adam knew she was right. When mom was depressed after Dad's death, she even cut Aunt Betsey out, without a word. And still, if she got into one of her dark moods, she would retreat into herself shutting everyone out again. But Aunt Betsey was loyal to Mom, through thick and thin. After Aunt Betsey's divorce was final, she moved here to Wilmington to be by Mom. They were so close, more like sisters than best friends. I explained to Aunt Betsey what I found here, which was basically nothing, and how that was the most concerning part. We both decided I should give it a little time, but if I hadn't heard from her by 9 pm, I would have to call the police.

Chapter 8

I stretched and looked at my watch.

The sun was starting to set, while I was lost in my memories. A few people passed by, hustling toward home or out to dinner. No one took notice of me or my tear-stained face.

I sat wondering how things turned out this way. Why was I alone here, sitting in this desolate town, no Thomas, no life, and presumably no sanity? How could I have ever thought that man today was actually Thomas? Thomas would never leave me alone like this! He would never leave me grieving for him. So, who was this man? This imposter, filling my mind with doubt and confusion. Opening up my festering wound, letting pain seep back into every crevice of my body. I didn't know who he was, and at this point, I didn't care anymore. I just wanted to be home, in my bed so that I could sleep. Blissful sleep, far away from the pain. Not to mention, Adam was probably wondering where I am. Waiting for me to come home and make him dinner. I started the car and headed for the highway. Driving past farm fields, gas stations, and the occasional lonesome car, I finally made it back to the interstate and headed for home.

I pulled into the driveway around 8:50 pm. Adam's car was still there. That boy must be hungry, I thought amusingly. Adam burst out the front door and headed straight for me.

"Mom! Where have you been?!" he shouted in my face. "I've been panic-stricken and worried about your safety! For god sake mom, you should have called me!"

I couldn't get a word in as he machine-gunned his frustration at me. When he finally settled down, I was able to speak.

"Adam, I left you a note that I went to run errands."

"Errands!? Since when do you run errands until 9 o'clock at night? And what note are you talking about? There was no note! Don't you care about anyone but yourself?" his face was red with anger. I felt ashamed, like a scolded child.

"I left you a note, Adam; I had no idea you'd be worried. And I'm sorry that I upset you, but I am a grown woman who can take care of herself!"

"Since when, Mom?" Adam retorted with such disdain; I knew it came from the heart.

I sat silently looking at him.

"I'm sorry, Mom, I didn't mean it," even though I knew he did. He wasn't done with me yet.

"I was extremely worried. Betsey was worried too; she said you stood her up today! She thought you were having one of your episodes."

Episodes? I thought bitterly. What do they know of my feelings or understand anything about me at all, I felt resentful.

"Well, I'm sorry I worried the two of you, but I'm tired now, and I want to go to bed," I said defiantly.

We stood there in the crisp night air which held the taste of approaching winter, with crickets still chirping in the distance. I was glad they were still around. There was always a comfort to the sound of them singing in the night air. Growing up in Boston, I had never heard a cricket chirp before. It was a sound I grew to love when I moved to the Carolinas.

Adam huffed and shrugged his shoulders. "Well, thanks a lot for wasting my night!"

What did he mean by wasting his night? There had been many a night he had stayed and hung out with me since he went off to school. Playing board games, watching tv, and just talking. Why was tonight such a waste?

"Adam, I really am sorry about this. I left the note so you wouldn't worry," I reached out and touched his arm gently.

He stared at me, with a look I had never seen on his face before. A look that said he'd had enough. He turned and walked toward his car.

"Get inside the house, Mom, and lock the door." He ordered. "I'll call you tomorrow," he said without looking back at me. And with that, he got into his car and drove away. I stood there for a moment watching his taillights disappear into the night. At that moment, I felt more alone than I had ever felt before.

I walked inside and shut the door. Sure enough, no note. I could've sworn I left it right there on the door. I looked around at the entrance to our home. Memories filled my heart and mind. Legos on the living room floor, RC cars screeching across the hardwood flooring, giggling boys upstairs. Nights and nights of movies, especially at our home in Marblehead, before Thomas died. We had family movie nights once a month, with candy and popcorn. Thomas and I would cuddle up on the couch, and the boys would sprawl out on the floor. One particular night we were watching an animated comedy, always animated for the boys, and

Thomas leaned over and whispered in my ear, "I love our life so much." And I couldn't have agreed more. We had so many wonderful nights before Thomas was gone. But once he was gone, so was the fun. I still tried to make it fun for the boys, but they knew my heart wasn't in it. And it just wasn't the same without their dad. For them or me.

I walked into the kitchen and opened the refrigerator. Sweet tea, Orange juice, V8, and milk. Boy, I must really like liquid nutrition, I almost laughed. On hard days like this, Thomas would always swoop in and take over for me, whipping up chocolate chip pancakes or his famous chili burgers. What I wouldn't give for a plate of chocolate chip pancakes and a side of Thomas right now.

I poured myself a glass of water before heading upstairs to bed. I walked up the stairs, and as I stepped on the sixth step, it creaked. Thomas said that was first on his to do list when we moved in. Adam had offered numerous times to repair it, but I wouldn't let him. In some twisted way, leaving it undone, kept a piece of Thomas with me.

I got undressed and slipped into my empty bed. Lying in the dark, all I could see were piercing blue eyes. At some point, I drifted off to sleep. I still saw the blue eyes, but they were different now, blood was pouring out of the corners of them. As I looked, the eyes weren't on sweet Thomas' face anymore; they were on a corpse, decayed, flesh falling off. I started screaming, and I woke myself up, still screaming.

Chapter 9

*I*t was now 9 o'clock in the morning. We had officially missed our flight. And I was really starting to worry. Where could he be? I asked the bellboy to put our bags in the storage closet while I went to look for Thomas some more. I couldn't keep him waiting with our stuff any longer. I walked around the main areas of the hotel again. Nothing. I went back to the room, and the maid was there outside the open door.

"Excuse me, have you seen the man who was staying here with me, my husband?"

She shook her head "No senora, I not see him today." She looked at me with caring eyes.

I peered past her into the room and saw the room looked just as it did the day we arrived. All traces of us were gone. Like we were never there.

I walked back down to the lobby and went up to the front desk. I was starting to feel a little nauseated. There was a line, the lady in front was complaining about her bill.

"I didn't order pay per view!" she screeched at the attendant.

"I don't even watch tv! And I'm not paying $25 for something I didn't order!" The attendant patiently listened to her go on and on for 10 minutes without interrupting. I was getting impatient though. Panic was starting to set in. I hadn't seen Thomas in hours. Where was he? He should be with me by now. Finally, the attendant said, "Let me get the manager and see what we can do. Please step to the side, and let me help these other guests while you wait. The manager will be able to help you in a moment." Once he returned from alerting the manager, he then dealt with a missing bag, a lost reservation, and a very long phone call inquiry about spa services. Finally, it was my turn.

"May I help you, ma'am?" the young dark-haired guy said with a cheerful voice, though the strain of the morning was showing on his face.

"Yes, I was wondering if there were any messages for me? My name is Sarah Avery."

He checked behind the counter for a moment and came back.

"I'm sorry, ma'am, but there are no messages for you."

My head started to spin, and I felt as if I might black out.

"Ma'am, are you okay?" he looked bewildered.

I looked at him with tears in my eyes.

"NO, I am not okay!" I shrieked.

"My husband is missing!"

The next few hours were a blur. A literal nightmare, filled with police, questions, detectives, more questions, news crews, and even more questions. And still no sign of Thomas. I was numb; this couldn't be real. Thomas was just here this morning. He was going to watch the sunrise, and go for a swim. Oh my god, go for a swim! My blood ran cold. I jumped up and ran out the back doors of the lobby, out to the beach, across the sand, and straight into the water.

I was screaming. "Oh my god Thomas!" "Thomas!" "THOMAS!" I collapsed in the water as I was being dragged back to shore.

The hotel put me in one of their small rooms located in the main building. The local doctor gave me a sedative to help calm me down. By this point, the entire facility was covered with police and reporters. Helicopters were flying overhead, and divers were searching the water. I curled up in a ball on the bed and cried until there were no more tears, only gut-wrenching sounds. I kept repeating the same words over and over.

"Thomas, where are you?" "Thomas please come back to me" "Thomas...."

A female detective had come earlier and asked for names and numbers of people to call. I gave them my parent's and Betsey's. Betsey was the only one who showed up. She was there the next morning when I awoke from a drug induced sleep.

"Betsey!" I collapsed into her arms and sobbed.

"It's okay darling; they're going to find him, I just know it." She stroked my hair and sat with me while I cried more.

Later, we went down to the lobby to check on the progress. By this point, they weren't calling him a missing person anymore. He was called "the drowning victim." I heard an officer say "the victim has been missing for over 24 hours and you know that current could take him all the way to Cuba. We most likely will never......"

He saw me standing there and stopped.

"Will never what?" I asked.

He just stared at me.

"Will never WHAT?" my voice was getting sharper and louder.

Betsey patted my back, "Settle down sweetie; they don't know anything yet."

I started to scream, "I SAID NEVER WHAT!?"

People in the lobby all stopped and stared. An older officer approached me, he took my hand and led me across to some brown faux leather chairs surrounded by plants in painted clay pots. We sat down across from each other. His face looked tired. I recognized him. He had been here since Thomas was reported as missing yesterday morning. He wiped his forehead with a handkerchief, while Mexican fiesta tunes played from an overhead speaker in the background.

"We didn't want to upset you any more than necessary, but I have to tell you that the chances of finding your husband's body, if he was actually lost in the ocean, are slim to none. We've had men searching for him for 18 hours straight, and we've come up emptyhanded. The way the current is pulling right now, it would be easy, even for the best swimmer to lose their strength in the water, and go under. The only other possibilities we have right now is the possibility of foul play or he just plain ran off. We are reviewing the security camera tapes right now in hopes of finding out what actually happened."

I was trying to digest what exactly he was saying to me. Drowning, foul play, ran off?

"He didn't run off, he loved m...e" my voice broke off.

"Wait, what do you mean by foul play?" my eyes were wide open in fear.

"It is highly unlikely at a resort like this, for anything to happen to one of the guests on site, but it is possible. Or it could be someone who knew him." His face was blank as he said those words.

I ran to the nearest trash can and threw up.

I spent five days in a Mexican interrogation room answering questions and crying. I was so numb from the pain; I wanted to curl up and die. Finally, after the American embassy intervened, I was cleared of all suspicion. They had reviewed the security cameras and saw Thomas go into the water and never come out. They searched for his body for three days and had given up the search. They said it was most likely his body would never be found. After I was cleared by the police investigation, I had to contend with the insurance investigator. Asking questions, I could not answer. I was exhausted in every possible way. The torture of them not finding Thomas' body, was nearly more than I could bear. I stayed as long I as could. But, I finally left for home after two weeks. I had been away from the boys for long enough. And I had to prepare a memorial service for Thomas. A memorial service with no body to bury. The flight home was long and arduous. Betsey had left a week earlier because she had to get back to her divorce proceedings. Her husband was being a real snake, even though he was the one who cheated. Betsey was such a sweetheart and deserved so much better. She was the only one who came to Mexico, telling me without saying a word, that she was the only one who truly cared. My parents threw money at the search and posted rewards for finding Thomas. They were sure he had run off, "those kinds of people always run off and abandon their families" they had said in an indignant tone when I was on the phone with them. It was so hurtful that they could defile Thomas' memory like that. He would never do that to his children, especially after what his father did to him. And I know that he loved us. He loved me; he knew how much I needed him. The plane touched down at ILM at 4 pm, and plane unloaded in an orderly fashion. I just sat in my seat, not even moving. Not ready to face reality. My new reality, a reality without Thomas.

Chapter 10

⚜

2016

$\mathcal{I}$ tossed and turned for the rest of the night. The nightmare had rattled my nerves, but honestly, I hadn't slept well since Thomas' death anyway. I went ahead and got up early, despite how tired I was. I made my way silently downstairs to make a cup of coffee. I used to love my mornings with Thomas. The early morning hours, when the boys were still asleep, belonged to us. We would sit together at our vintage round wooden kitchen table, and make idle conversation. Neither of us was exactly morning people, but we were happy to just to be together. Thomas would always lean over the table and kiss my cheek. "Good morning, beautiful!" he would say. Even when he went through the tough times, he always said it, every morning; despite my bed head, faded nightgowns, and morning breath. He said it, and I knew he meant it. We would drink steamy coffee and eat our breakfast together. Our little sacred routine. Then the day would begin. Thomas rushing off to shower and get to the office and me getting the boys up. Making Captain Crunch filled bowls and packing lunches.

Those were the happiest moments of my life. You never realize how much the little things are really the big things, until they're gone.

I went out onto the back deck that overlooked the pool. Birds were chirping and jumping around in my newly planted flower garden. The air was fresh and smelled of honeysuckles. My robe kept the slight chill in the air away from me. The pool was due to be winterized. I wondered if I would even bother to have it set up next year. I had kept the pool going, with the help of a pool company, every year. The boys used it when they were younger. Even through high school, they still used it. Their friends would come over, and they would spend hours out there. Thomas would've been glad it was being used, but now it just sat there year after year. I was never much of a swimmer. Both of my brothers were on the swim team when I was little, natural born swimmers. My parents urged me to try, but I was never that fond of being in the water. I was afraid. I had terrifying nightmares for as long as I could remember, of being surrounded by a wide body of water in the dark, and no shoreline in sight. Because of the dreams, I was always uneasy around water.

I sipped my coffee and wondered about the man I saw yesterday. I wish I could've gotten a better look at him. If I hadn't panicked and fainted, I could have better analyzed what I really saw. My cheeks flushed with embarrassment of the memory. I made such a scene. So many people were around me, good grief. I bet they were still talking about the incident today. Anyway, if it had been Thomas, wouldn't he have recognized me too? I sat and laughed out loud at the foolishness of my notion and decided to put it to rest. Or so I thought.

I went inside and called Betsey.

"Hi..." I said sheepishly.

"Well, hello there stranger," Betsey said lightly.

She never held a grudge.

"I'm sorry about yesterday, Adam told me you were worried."

"It's okay Sarah, you know me, I go with the flow."

Betsey was loyal, through thick and thin. She had remarried a few years ago. A dentist, his name was Jack, and he was crazy about her. He was ten years older than she was. She was really happy, and I was happy for her. Once she got rid of that cheating first husband, Betsey really blossomed. We had been friends for years. I met her right after we moved back to Boston. I was doing wedding announcements, and she was a disgruntled bride. I had misspelled her fiancé's name in the paper. His name was Shane, and I had published Shame. Shame Smith...... She came up to the paper and demanded to speak to me. She came right up to my desk to inform me about my blunder, and when she said "you called my husband Shame" she began laughing hysterically, and I could not help but start laughing too. We were instant friends. She felt like the sister that I never had. She was an only child and felt the same about me. We had been super close all these years. We still laugh about how Shane really turned out to be Shame after all. She's the only person I didn't shut out completely after what happened to Thomas. I debated whether I should tell her about what happened.

"Betsey, what would you say if I told you I thought I saw Thomas yesterday?"

She sat silently for a moment.

"I'm sure that happens all the time to people who lose someone they love; the mind puts that person in their environment because the pain is so great."

It was feasible what she was saying, but I still couldn't shake the piercing blue eyes.

"Betsey, he had the same eyes...."

I could hear her breathing; she must be weighing her words carefully.

Finally, she said, "Sarah, do you need me to come over?"

"No, no I'm fine, really," I lied.

Betsey paused. "Sarah, you know that wasn't really Thomas, don't you?"

"Of course, I do!" I lied again.

"Okay..." she said with obvious hesitation. "Please call me later, if you need me, sweetie." I hung up lecturing myself.

Not Thomas, not Thomas, not Thomas.

Though I did realize the sheer impossibility of it being Thomas, the thought ate at me the rest of the day like a cancer. As I went about my errands, I found myself looking for him. At the dry cleaners, the bank, and even at the grocery store. As if I expected him to step out of the cereal aisle and back into my arms. Every time I saw a man with dark brown hair, my heart would stop for a moment. And with the realization that it was indeed not him, the foolishness of my thoughts would harass me. I am ridiculously insane, I thought. Why was I torturing myself? No matter how much I wanted it to be Thomas, I couldn't force it to be him. My sheer will couldn't bring him back into reality. If it could, he would have never disappeared in the first place. And anyway, I was looking for Thomas as he was 14 years ago. He would have aged by now. I mean, I certainly didn't look the same as I did back then. Suddenly it occurred to me, that was it!! Obviously, he didn't recognize me! And the notion soon grew larger and soon became a solid belief. I was then consumed with the thought, with the belief, that it was Thomas after all.

I was no longer a grieving wife. I was possessed with the notion that he was alive. My Thomas was alive and walking the streets of Wilmington. I suddenly paused. I felt tears start to sting my eyes. Where has he been for 14 years!? How could he have just left us here like that, with no word that he was okay? But my heart raced with anticipation, the only thing that really mattered now, is that he was back. There was just one thing to do. I had to find him again. But how? My mind raced. How would I ever be able to track him down? It occurred to me that I needed to go back to where I saw him. I wondered if I really did expect him to just miraculously appear in the same location again? I didn't know, but I was prepared to find out. I had nothing to lose and everything to gain. All rational thinking was gone. I grabbed my sunglasses for a flimsy disguise and drove back to Olde Towne Square. After all, no one would believe me, the crazy lady. I would have to get the proof myself.

So, I began my stakeout. I was consumed, maybe even deranged with the thought of seeing him again. I spent my days sitting in my car just opposite People's bank. The place where I last saw him. At first, my energy was high, and I was on fire with anticipation. I pictured myself as a detective in one of those late night black and white movies. Movies that kept me going all those sleepless nights after Thomas died. Each day I ate my packed lunch, did crossword puzzles, and watched the front of the bank. I saw hundreds, maybe thousands of people going in and coming out of the bank all day long. The days were warm, and I had to keep my windows rolled down to keep me somewhat cool. I watched seagulls flying over, people walking dogs, tourists gazing and gasping at all the sights that I now take for granted. I wondered what they saw that was so fascinating?

All the sitting and waiting was making me crazier than when I started out. I was starting to wonder when I should give up. It had been four consecutive days, 43 hours and 32 minutes, of this monotony and the excitement, were wearing thin. I began talking to the little birds hopping around and eating the crumbs on the sidewalk. I was singing Broadway tunes to myself, even though I didn't know most of the words. People would stare at me as they walked by. I didn't care. I'd lost all sense of dignity. I was stalking my dead husband. How much lower or crazier can you go? The minutes ticked by slowly. I found myself glazing over and not being able to focus on the people as they passed by. Suddenly there was a knock on my windshield. I nearly jumped out of my skin and gave a little shriek. My autonomy in my little Volvo universe had been disrupted. I looked up to see a uniformed officer.

"Ma'am, may I ask what you are doing here?" His face was not friendly.

"I...I...umm.... was just sitting here to get some quiet... ummm.. away from the kids, brought a snack and all..."

I laughed nervously and lifted my lunch bag to show him. I couldn't believe how easily the lies were sliding out of my mouth lately.

He was a little on the chubby side and had snow white hair. He leaned closer to my window and looked at me disapprovingly.

"Well, you can't sit outside of a bank for hours, and not raise suspicion. Not to mention there's a time limit on parking here." He pointed at the parking sign, and his face was stone cold, despite the smile I was giving him.

"I would strongly recommend a new location for your relaxation time." He smiled that time, but I could sense a feeling of distrust in his tone.

I started to say something else; then I saw what I had been waiting to see for 14 years. It was like he had magically appeared out of a dream. Walking down the street toward People's bank. He was whistling. Just like Thomas used to do. Always whistling. The officer was still talking, but I couldn't hear him any longer. All I could see, hear, or feel was my Thomas. He was wearing a blue button-up shirt with the sleeves rolled up, and khaki dress slacks. He looked different now. His hair was lighter, but I knew it was him. I knew that body; I knew that face. I got out of my car and ran toward him, not looking back at the officer, or my open door.

Chapter 11

Adam picked up the phone, lost in thought. *I really need to apologize to Mom. I don't know why I flipped out on her like that. I think this thing with Emily is starting to get to me. I have to tell Mom as soon as possible. I really think she would like Emily. I mean, what's not to like? She is such an amazing girl. Long legs, long hair, great sense of humor, loves baseball, I mean this girl is the bomb, and she likes me, she likes me a lot.*

Just then Emily came up behind me and gave me a squeeze. "What are you thinking about, sexy?"

She was wearing nothing but my shirt, and she was calling *me* sexy.

"I'm getting ready to call my mom; I was really hard on her the other day," I said ashamedly.

"Well then call her already, you only have one mom for crying out loud!" she slapped me on the arm.

She could be pretty blunt sometimes, but that was part of her charm.

I dialed mom's number, and it went straight to voicemail.

"What the hell?!"

I was instantly irritated. What was going on with mom lately? Something was definitely not right. I hoped she wasn't having a break down again. She's been doing pretty okay lately. But who knows.... Maybe she's met a man, and she doesn't want me to know. Wouldn't that be hilariously ironic? Us both hiding something like that from each other....

Right then, my phone dinged with a message from Blake.

"What's up bro?" his usual greeting.

I texted back my usual "Not much, what's up with you?"

The message said read, but he wasn't typing back. 15 minutes passed. Strange, he must have gotten distracted. But as soon as I had given up on waiting for a response, Coldplay's Viva la Vida starting playing, my ringtone.

It was Blake.

"Hey brother, what's up!?"

Does he not have another greeting to use? I thought, getting even more irritated.

"Not much, how about you?" Damn, I was guilty of it too.

Blake paused "How's mom?" I was shocked, he rarely asked about mom.

"She's....well.... okay, I guess. Why?" I had no intention of telling him about her recent antics.

"This is going to sound really dumb, but I had this dream about her last night."

This immediately sparked the psychologist in me.

"What was the dream about, Blake?" I prodded.

"Well...she was chasing someone, and she kept calling out Dad's name," he stopped speaking.

"Anything else happen?" I encouraged him to go on.

"Yeah, she caught up with the person, and she grabbed his arm. He looked just like Dad from behind, but when he turned around, he had no face, and she started screaming this horrific scream, and I woke up. It just really freaked me out, and I wanted to make sure she was okay."

He paused and then said, "Adam, I feel guilty sometimes about not staying in touch with her. I just can't relate to her at all, but dammit, I do love her!"

"Hey Blake, don't worry, she knows that!" I said to only soothe his justified guilt.

His dream was stereotypical Cathartic dream, but I know it had genuinely freaked him out for him to call me about it. He knew I'd over analyze it and he hated when I did that.

"Hey, don't worry about mom so much, I've got it under control here," I lied.

"Yeah, *you always have,*" Blake said with a touch of resentment in his voice.

"Hey, you know you could always come and visit her. She'd like that." I added to send a sting back his way.

"Yeah, maybe I will.... I don't know.... I *would* like for you guys to meet Becca."

"Come anytime brother, we both miss you!" and I meant it. I missed my brother a lot.

I didn't tell him about Emily. He was so self-absorbed, he wouldn't have really cared anyway. If he ends up coming, which I doubt he will, I will introduce her to him then. But, I had to tell mom about Emily soon. Emily has mentioned it a few times too. I think she's starting to get a little mad about it. She might be an awesome cool girl, but she's still a girl, and they can be pretty nasty when they're mad. I certainly didn't want her ticked at me. After all, I had met her parents a couple of weeks ago. She jokingly asked me the other day, if I was ashamed of her. But behind every joke, is always a thread of truth, and I knew my time was running out. I was definitely not ashamed of her. I just needed to find the right time. My mom was fragile, and I didn't want to rock the boat. And on top of that, I'm still trying to figure out what was going on with her lately and why she wasn't answering her phone anymore.

I looked over at Emily, still in my shirt, lying on my couch, reading a Michael Crichton novel. My heart gave a little start. Oh my god, I think I might really love this girl. I went over to her and started gently rubbing the inside of her thigh. She put down her book and looked at me, that move gets to her every time. I slid over a little closer and started to kiss her. And then my phone started playing Viva la Vida again.

"Ughhhhhhhhh!" I was not happy.

I got up and went to grab my phone.

"Where are you going?" she asked with a purr in her voice.

"I will be right back; don't you go anywhere!" I winked at her and picked up the phone.

It was mom, and she was hysterical.

"Adam.... Adam.... You have to come home now!"

I looked over at Emily and sighed. "I'm sorry babe, but I gotta go."

"Oh, you're such a tease!" she said with a laugh.

I kissed her again, but briefly, and was out the door.

Chapter 12

I lost all care and concern about the officer behind me, my open car door with purse inside, the people around me, all staring at me, the crazed woman running down the street. All I could see was Thomas. He didn't see me though. As I ran toward him, time slowed, as if I was in a dream and my feet weren't moving normally. I felt as if I was running through quicksand. Finally, as my feet reached the other side of the street, my body caught up with my brain. Thomas was directly in front of me. He was walking along all alone, just steps ahead of me. I finally got close enough to reach out and touch his arm. He turned around to see who touched him.

"Thomas!?"

I said as I looked at an older but still handsome Thomas Avery.

"Excuse me?" he replied, looking around nervously.

"Thomas...it's me, Sarah...."

He looked at me blankly.

"I'm sorry, I'm not who you are looking for."

A knot came up in my throat.

"but Thomas........*it is you*.... I would know *you* anywhere."

He stared at me with a look of steel.

"You said your name is Sarah? You actually do look a little familiar to me."

"Yes, I'm Sarah!" I stammered. My brain was whirling. What was happening? This was Thomas standing here in front of me, yet he was saying he wasn't Thomas. And he doesn't even know who I am!

"Thomas.... why don't you know me?!" I said as I nearly choked on my words. I could feel the redness in my face.

His face softened, and he touched my hand. "Hey now.... everything is going to be okay."

I started to cry, quietly at first, but then came a full out sob.

He stepped closer and touched my shoulder.

"Sarah, is there anyone I can call for you?"

I didn't answer. I just kept crying, and he started looking around, I presumed for someone to rescue him out of this awkward situation, but his eyes didn't look annoyed at all. They looked kind and maybe even a little nervous, but most of all they looked like Thomas.

"Let's grab you a water here, and we can talk for a minute," he said as he led me onto the outdoor patio at Lila's Bistro.

This little place was usually bustling with business, but we had caught it during the in between hours. After lunch, and before the dinner rush. He guided me to a seat under a brightly colored umbrella.

"Why don't you sit here for a moment and I'll be right back."

I sat there at the metal mesh table in a daze, while people walked by me, caught up in their normal everyday life. Life was moving forward, while I sat there in a whirlwind of emotion and confusion. I often wondered so many times after Thomas disappeared, how the world was still moving forward when mine was forever destroyed. How could the earth not just spin right off of its axis? I had resented others for their happiness, walking around in their oblivion while my heart was ripped from my chest. And I was feeling that again now. Except now instead of grief, I was so confused; so lost. What was happening to me?

Maybe I had stepped into some alternate universe where Thomas and I had never met. Maybe I was completely crazy, and none of this was actually happening. The latter theory began to ring true when I realized it had been several minutes since he had stepped inside of the bistro. I instantly thought, I really did imagine it. I was running around talking to someone who wasn't there. I tried to see into the bistro windows, but the glare just created a mirror. I could feel my heart rate rising. Panic was starting to set in. Then just like out a dream, he stepped out of the door carrying a bottle of water and a glass. Lime Perrier, my favorite. Of course, he would remember.

"I wasn't sure what kind of water to get you, and the girl inside said she had served you before. She said you always ordered this. I hope she was right." He smiled nervously at me.

I wondered what he was thinking.

"Yes, she is right," I said with a dejected tone.

I took the Perrier and filled my glass, wondering if the girl inside was calling the wacky wagon to come pick me up. I could picture him in there, telling her about the psychotic woman outside and telling her to call 911. That's probably really why he brought me here, to get rid of me. I thought about the officer that I ran off from; he would be all too happy to testify about my abnormal behavior.

I seriously thought about running away from here, from him. But then I looked at Thomas, and I was frozen in my seat.

"You know, I think I do remember who you are, aren't you the one who fainted in the street earlier in the week?" He smiled so sweetly that my heart swelled with happiness.

Wait, did he say 'the lady who fainted'? What was going on? Why doesn't he remember me, why doesn't he remember us?

"Yes, that's me." I felt my face redden.

"So, tell me about this Thomas you're looking for," he said with a soft smile.

"But...*but you...are*," I whispered.

He stopped me.

"I'm very sorry, Sarah, but I am not Thomas. My name is Collin Young. I just moved here, from California. I lived there for years, but am certainly enjoying North Carolina. I am a real estate agent." He smiled with pride.

I sat in disbelief, listening to him speak.

"I moved here because I had spent some time on the east coast when I was younger, and I was itching to get back, but the timing had to be right to make such a big move. But, you know how that goes," he said with a tentative laugh.

I was sure that he was still unsure about my mental stability.

He saw by my face that I wasn't buying it. He reached into his pocket and pulled something out and placed it on the table. A California driver's license. His picture, with the name Collin Young.

"But you look just like him......" I trailed off.

He touched my hand again for the second time, but this time I noticed much more intently. His touch warmed me immediately.

"He was my husband, and he disappeared.... well actually, he died....14 years ago."

Was I really telling Thomas his own story?

"I'm really sorry about your loss, Sarah. And I'm really sorry that seeing me opened up your pain."

"Opened up my pain?" I said sharply, immediately regretting my tone.

"I have never stopped loving......." I started to cry softly.

He kept his hand on mine for a moment, and then pulled it away. His face looked pained. I didn't know what else to say. How could I convince him?

He tried to make idle conversation.

"Did you know that someone tried to rob The People's Bank right before you fainted? I was talking to some of the bystanders when I saw you. The police apprehended the guy immediately. The police response was great."

"Really?" I feigned interest. The only thing on my mind was Thomas. He didn't attempt to say anything else.

We sat together for a while in an awkward silence.

I'm not sure how much time had passed when he finally said. "Sarah, are you okay?"

"Yes," I said sharply.

I felt flustered and angry. I stood up from the table.

There was nothing else to be said. I was devastated.

He stood up too, and reached into his pocket and withdrew a leather wallet. I watched as his familiar hands opened the wallet. He put his license back inside and then pulled out a card.

"Here's my business card. If you are ever in need of a real estate agent...." he trailed off.

I took the card, and we walked together for a short distance. He turned to me.

"It was nice meeting you, Sarah. Again, I'm sorry that seeing me upset you, that was not my intention."

I muttered.... "It's okay."

I didn't understand what was going on with Thomas but fighting him wasn't going to help.

He turned and walked away. I stood there and watched him until he disappeared from sight, with my heart caught in my throat. I started to wonder again if I had imagined the whole thing. It was all too bizarre to be real. Impossible that it would be my Thomas and him deny me, and himself, for that matter. Thomas was so solid, always prepared, and most of all, protective of me. He would never do this to me. My thoughts ran wild. But who or what had I seen, if it wasn't Thomas. Was I just having a conversation with myself? Did I even drink a Perrier? My head started to spin, and I started to mentally commit to the possibility of insanity. I squeezed my hands into fists, and I felt tears burning down my face. But then I felt something sharp in my hand. I looked down, and I was holding a business card.

Collin Young, Real Estate Professional.

Chapter 13

⟨※⟩

*A*dam pulled into the driveway of his childhood home, not knowing what to expect. Mom had sounded so upset on the phone, nearly hysterical. Very different than the normal monotone banter that she usually had these days. She was almost like a robot. She rarely showed any emotion at all. So, what was going on?! My thoughts raced around trying to piece together an explanation. I always had the answer. That's me, old reliable Adam. So, what could it be? Then my heart began to race. A terrible thought occurred to me. Oh my god....... Noooo, I didn't want to think, to know. What if she's sick? Maybe that's why she's been acting this way. Maybe she was gone having tests done in Raleigh the day I got so mad at her? My thoughts ran wild. I didn't know what I'd do if lost her too. My heart clenched with preemptive grief. The thought spurred my motion into overdrive. I nearly ran from the car to the front door and stepped inside the house. Every light was off making things even eerier.

"Mom!?" I almost shrieked.

She didn't answer, but I heard crying coming from the kitchen. I walked into the room tentatively and turned on the light.

She was sitting on the floor with an open bottle of wine. No glass. And she was clutching her wedding picture.

***

I heard the front door open, and Adam call my name. I couldn't even respond. The tears were coming, and they wouldn't stop. I heard his panic, but I just sat there. I couldn't move or speak. The sedatives that I took before I opened the bottle of wine, had started to kick in. I ignored the rule of never mixing pills with alcohol. The prescription said "as needed," and boy they were needed!

He came into the kitchen where I sat on the floor face to face with my antique white custom cabinetry. Pull out shelves and drawers for every opening. The sales guy promised this would meet all my kitchen needs. I hadn't even opened one of these lower cabinets since putting in unused kitchen appliances, pans, and dishes. I couldn't remember the last time that I actually even made a meal for myself. The only time I cook is for Adam. And that is usually spaghetti or meatloaf. His favorites. Meals that didn't require anything special. I had all this specialty kitchen stuff from when Thomas was with me.

Woks, food processors, Bundt pans, Corningware. He loved to cook and so did I. I saved all of it, just like all the other unused items around this house. All waiting for Thomas to reappear somehow. I started to cry even harder. I thought about those months after moving here to Wilmington and how angry I was at Thomas for leaving me. How could he just die and leave me behind? And not even give me a body to bury.

"Mom!" Adam knelt down beside me.

"Mom, are you okay?" he questioned.

My sobs were all he got in return.

66

"Mom, please tell me what's wrong...." he sounded really upset.

I looked up at my son; he had such care and concern for me. I guzzled down what was left in the bottle and hiccupped a little. I was drunk. Okay, very drunk. Tears were running down my face. Why was I crying? I couldn't remember now. My thoughts were getting jumbled up. I felt dizzy. Nothing made sense. Wait. Why was Adam here anyway? I think I called him, maybe. Yes, I did call him. I wonder what I said? I started to giggle, and then it turned into a full out laugh. I couldn't help it. Adam's face changed from concern to anger. I was laughing out loud now, despite all of the confusion. I was laughing.

"Mom! Are you drunk!?" Adam almost snarled at me.

I stopped laughing immediately. Adam was angry. Why was he being so mean? I started to cry again. My head felt heavy. My thoughts grew fuzzier.

"Really!?" Adam muttered to himself.

"Come on Mom, let's get you to bed!"

He took the photo I had been clutching and set it down.

Then he grunted as he tried to lift me to my feet.

I dropped the wine bottle just as he lifted me, and it shattered all over the floor.

"Dammit!" he yelled.

I could barely stand up, my legs felt like jello. I felt overwhelmed with sleepiness. I could barely keep my eyes open.

"I want to go home," I said with a slur that sounded perfectly spoken to my inebriated ears.

All I wanted was to get into my bed and sleep. Where was Thomas? I couldn't remember now. I started to panic. I tried to pull away from Adam's grip.

"Mom! Knock it off!"

He held me tighter as we made it to the top of the stairs. He led me into my room.

"Thomas!" I yelled into the dark empty room.

"Oh my god, where's Thomas!?"

I looked wildly at Adam. There were 2 of him now.

"Do you mean dad? He's not here mom. He has never been." Adam said soulfully.

I immediately slapped him across the face. He was a liar! He looked at me stunned like he didn't know what had just happened. Who does he think he is?! How dare he lie to me about something like that!

He lifted me up and got me into bed. I rolled over and whispered. "When you find Thomas tell him I'm waiting...." And I fell into a deep dreamless sleep.

***

Adam closed the door hoping his mother would stay asleep. The frustration at her was only overpowered by the nagging thought of why she was acting this way lately. She never got drunk, another new behavior for her this week. And why did she slap me!? That hurt. I can't believe that she put her hands on me! She was not a mom who spanked. Dad handled the discipline when we were little, and after he died, the most punishment we ever got was a short grounding. And now she had just slapped me, and hard too. And why is she asking for dad like that, and not even referring to him as Dad? Just Thomas. I wondered about her current mental state. We always teased her about being crazy, but this was serious. Her quirky behavior was harmless in the past, but this unpredictable behavior and the delusional things she was saying was very concerning. We learned about Delusional Disorder in school. It could be as simple as Post Traumatic Stress. I didn't know. She was acting a little different from the normal diagnosed patient, but she would need to see a doctor soon if she didn't snap out of this.

I walked into the kitchen and looked at the broken glass all over the floor. I sighed. I could've had a fantastic night with Emily, and here I am babysitting my drunk mom. I went into the pantry and got the broom and dustpan. As I came out, I saw the pills. Ativan. I wondered if she had taken any tonight? That would certainly explain some of her behavior tonight. She was blitzed. She wouldn't even remember any of this tomorrow.

Viva la Vida started to play. I picked it up; it was Emily.

"Hello," I said in a hushed tone. I was little afraid mom would wake back up.

"Hi, babe. Is everything okay there?" she sounded concerned.

"Yeah, my mom just had a little too much to drink, and was feeling sad." I downplayed it intentionally.

"Oh, poor thing." Emily sounded genuinely sad. She had a tender heart.

Of course, she had no idea how my mom was acting tonight. I would not be telling her either. Way too embarrassing!

"It's okay; she's asleep now. But, I'm going to hang out here for a bit just to make sure she doesn't need anything."

"Okay, that's a good idea. But, I won't be here when you get back. I have to get back home to study."

Dammit! I was hoping to go home and pick up where I left off before I came here.

"Okay, I'll call you tomorrow then," I gave in return; I wasn't going to beg her to stay.

"Okay, sounds good! Goodnight Adam." Even her voice was sexy.

I put the phone down and swept up all the glass. Then, I picked up mom's wedding photo. She was smiling so big, looking up at dad. I couldn't even remember the last time I saw her genuinely smile. She was wearing a long flowing white dress. Simple, not like the kind you see on those magazine covers. She had flowers in her hair. Her hair was down and blowing in the wind. She said she loved this pose because it wasn't a pose at all. It was a snapshot of life. A moment captured, she said. Dad was wearing a casual white shirt untucked with khaki pants. I looked like him a lot in this photo. He wasn't much older than me when this was taken. I wondered what he would look like now. I still missed him so much. I know he would have liked Emily. He would definitely approve. Especially since she loves baseball like us. I set the photo back up on the shelf from where she had taken it down from. I didn't want to leave it out just in case the delusions weren't pills and alcohol induced after all. I hung out for about hour reading useless posts on social media. Then I went upstairs and peeked in on her. She hadn't moved at all, but she was snoring. Man, she really was messed up. Good grief.

I locked up the house and headed home. As I was driving, I thought about Blake's dream. He said Mom was chasing someone calling out dad's name....and a cold chill went down my spine.

Chapter 14

❦

I woke up with a pounding headache. The kind that makes you not want to open your eyes again...ever.

I had a hangover for sure. The last time I can ever remember having a hangover like this one was on Thomas, and I's 5th wedding anniversary. We had gone out to a Mexican Restaurant and ate Fajitas coupled with several margaritas each. Then on a whim, we bought a bottle of tequila and a bag of limes, on the way home. We paid the babysitter, put the boys to bed, and then took shots of tequila followed by lime wedges until well after midnight. We were acting like silly kids. He brought our cd player outside and set it on the patio, and then he put on some Jimmy Buffet. We pretended we were in the islands on vacation. We laughed so much that night. We danced together under the stars. Then we made love on a blanket. We fell asleep out there like that. We both woke up with pretty severe hangovers and stiff bodies at dawn, from sleeping on the ground all night. Neither of us was big drinkers, so we paid extra when we had a little too much. Yet Thomas still took care of me, despite his throbbing headache and aching body. He brought me a freshly made Bloody Mary. He gently pushed my hair out of my eyes, and kissed me on the forehead and said, "Good Morning, Beautiful!"

That memory stung extra hard this morning. But in reality, no matter what was going on in my life, good or bad, I could always find a way to bring it back to Thomas. Maybe it was a coping mechanism, or maybe it was a way I found to secretly feel sorry for myself. Although I had been accused of that many times by my parents, I would never admit it out loud. Missing Thomas had become part of who I am now. I don't think anything could ever change that.

I tried to remember what I did last night. I was pretty upset when I got home about seeing Thomas, Thomas' twin, or whoever the hell he was. This whole situation had me unglued.

I remember taking the pill and opening the bottle of wine. I have no idea what happened after that. I was embarrassed but thankful that no one knew but me.

I went into the kitchen to find some ibuprofen. I poured myself the last of the orange juice into a tall glass and tossed the carton into the trash can. Just before the lid closed, I saw broken glass. I opened it back up and peered inside. I don't remember breaking that bottle. I looked around the kitchen to see what else was amiss. Nothing. Oh well, I thought dismissively. At least no one knows the condition I was in last night.

I went into the living room and sat down on the couch. I hoped this headache would go away soon. I needed to get to the grocery store and buy a few things today. My cell phone started ringing, making my head throb even more. I drug myself off the couch as much to make the phone stop making noise as anything else. It was Betsey.

I answered and tried to sound as lively as possible.

"Sarah!" Betsey was nearly yelling.

"Yes?" I answered reluctantly; I was not in the mood for drama this morning.

"You know how you told me that you saw Thomas!?" her voice was shaking.

I had not heard Betsy this amped up in a long time.

"Of course, I remember, why?" My head was pounding, and I wanted to get off the phone.

"I think that I saw him too!" she nearly shouted.

"Oh my god, are you serious!?" my heart started racing, and I no longer had a headache. I guess adrenaline really is the cure for everything.

"Yes, Sarah, I am sure that I saw him. But yet, it wasn't him. He said his name was Collin Young, but Oh my god, I swear it was Thomas!"

Her voice was in that high pitch it gets when she's really happy or really angry. I was so happy that someone other than me had seen him! I wasn't crazy after all!

"Betsey, where did you see him? You actually talked to him!?" I bulleted out questions. I needed to know everything.

"Well, you know my annoying neighbors Tim and Carol Langston? They are moving, thank god. And early this morning they had a real estate agent over there. I saw his car parked in the driveway and of course, I was being nosy, as usual. And this guy walked out to his car to get the For Sale sign to put out in their yard. When he turned around, I saw him! I ran right out the door, in my robe and all, right up to him. He turned toward me, smiled and said 'Hello' like he didn't know me. Then I said, 'Hi Thomas!' And he just looked at me, and for a second I thought he was angry, or something, and then he said 'That's so weird, that's the second time I've gotten that this week.' I immediately felt ridiculous standing out there in my robe just staring at him like a deer in the headlights.

He held out his hand to me and said 'I'm Collin Young.' I told him, 'I'm so sorry for the confusion,' and went back into the house, but Sarah, oh my god, he looks just like him, I mean a little different but the similarities are uncanny! He is a little older, but I swear it could be him!"

I felt a knot rise up in my throat and I slid to the floor.

"I told you Betsey!" choking back tears.

"I know you did sweetheart, but I mean how could I have believed you? But I'm so sorry I didn't..."

I knew she truly felt bad about not just trusting me in the first place.

"Betsey, I tracked him down and talked to him too."

I couldn't begin to tell her that I stalked him for four days.

"I just don't know what to do, he doesn't remember me, or he's choosing to act like he doesn't. Either way, I don't know what to do." I said gloomily.

Betsey chuckled.

"Well, it seems to me that you might want to get some information about listing your house for sale. I mean, there is a mighty cute new real estate agent in the area!"

"Oh my god, you are a genius, Betsey! I mean, he did give me his business card."

"Well, there you go! I say give him a call, and soon!"

"I will call him. But Betsey, I'm scared..."

"Scared is okay, I would be too. But on the bright side, you already lost Thomas once, so you can't lose him again."

She had no idea about what she was saying, and I knew better than that. I was already in anguish. I was being tormented ever since that day I first saw him again. This situation had danger written all over it.

"Thanks for everything Bets! I will keep you posted."

"You better!" she retorted with a laugh.

We hung up, and I went upstairs to get a shower. I had to think. Think. Having him come here? To our house? I didn't know if I was ready, but at the same time, all I could think about was his face, his hands, his mouth on mine. My whole body shook at the memory of his touch.

What I wouldn't give for it to be Thomas. Thomas here again, in my arms, in my bed. Waking up to his face every morning. Kissing his lips every night. I would give anything. Anything at all.

I got out of the shower and dried my hair. Another drawback of cutting it off. I lost the ability to just get out of the shower and let it air dry. After the arduous task of drying and straightening my hair into a picture-perfect bob. I put on white shorts and a navy blue striped tee shirt. Threw on my sandals and went out the door to shop.

There was a farmer's co-op just down the street from my house. I really enjoyed buying local fresh produce, eggs, and meat. It was something Thomas, and I did every Saturday when we lived in Marblehead. We always went down to the local farmer's market. The boys loved it. The market was always busy with vendors selling freshly made items. Local honey, hand churned butter, fresh cream, jarred pickles, homemade soaps, melons, a thousand pepper varieties, and so much more. I never wanted to leave, and we always came home with plenty. I loved to buy flowers and strawberries in the spring. Apples and homemade pumpkin pie in the fall. The farmer's co-op was similar to the farmer's market. It wasn't the same, but that was okay with me. And I still got to buy fresh local foods, what little I actually ate. It was one of the routines that helped keep me sane.

I drove up to the parking lot of the farmer's co-op. The place was packed. I wasn't thrilled at the crowd but made my way inside anyway. I walked down aisles filled with herbal remedies, dried seasonings, skin products in mason jars, and hand sewn towels. I loved the smells. So fresh and clean. I was lost in my own thoughts, as people bumped into me and then pushed around me.

I thought of Thomas. Memories flooded my mind. His hand in mine while we walked together. The smell of his hair after a shower. His toned body working in the yard. He was one of the few men in our neighborhood that could still take his shirt off while working.

I knew all the wives had their noses against the window panes when he was out there shirtless. And he was mine, all mine. I don't know why my mind kept going back to his body. Even though it had been 14 years since I had been with a man, I usually didn't struggle with it.

"Well hello there!" someone said behind me.

I nearly screamed I was so startled. I turned around and there he was standing in front of me. Thomas. I felt my face burning, wondering if he could read my thoughts. I dropped my basket of strawberries, and they spilled out rolling all over the floor.

I bent over and started picking them up. He knelt down to grab the empty basket and help me.

"How are you?" he looked at me as he was picking up the strawberries.

"Ummm.... okay...." I laughed nervously.

I was taken so off guard. I never expected to see him here. But of course, he would love this place.

We gathered all the strawberries up into the basket again. He handed me the basket.

"Thank you...." I stammered.

"I'm sorry I spilled them. You really startled me!"

I looked down at my feet and my unpainted toenails.

"I'm sorry I scared you," he half laughed. "I don't know a lot of people here yet and was happy to see a familiar face."

Oh my gosh, he was so handsome. Still so handsome. I looked at him in his button-up shirt and khaki pants and couldn't help but wonder if he had that same toned body like before. I blushed again. I had to get it together.

"It's okay. Apparently, I startle easily." I tried to laugh.

"So, are you feeling better? I mean from yesterday? You were pretty upset." He looked at me intently.

I had a decision to make. He was standing here talking to me. Clearly, he wasn't trying to avoid the "crazy lady." I didn't want to run him off with my intense accusations of who he actually was. So, I played along. What could it hurt? Playing pretend with a look-alike Thomas.

"Actually, I was going to call you...." I said nonchalantly.

"Really!?" his face lit up with a genuine smile.

"I wanted you to come by and give me your thoughts on our, I mean my house and its market value."

"You know, I'd love to do that for you. But I couldn't help but secretly hope you were calling to ask me out on a date."

I felt my cheeks burning. What the heck was wrong with me? I don't think I have ever blushed this much in my life. Even when I was an awkward teenager and Seth Collins asked me to Junior Prom. I had a crush on him for months, and when he finally asked me to prom, I nearly came out of my skin. He turned out to be such a creep. When my girlfriends and I played MASH, his name was always my first choice for marriage along with Rob Lowe and Corey Hart. Man, was I ever glad that MASH had no real predictability of the future. Otherwise, I would be driving a pink jeep, have 15 children, be unhappily married to Seth and working as a Rocket Scientist.

"A date?" I could not help but give a nervous giggle.

"But, hey, I'll take looking at your house, if it means I get to see you again!" he winked at me, and my toes curled up with joy.

Game face, game face. I kept telling myself.

"So, when do you want me to come by?"

"Today, tomorrow, any time...." I could not complete my sentence. My thoughts were running wild.

He just kept smiling. And oh, he still had that famous Thomas Avery smile. That was why his business was such a success. People liked Thomas, and they trusted him. He would never do wrong by anyone.

"Today then?" I couldn't believe I had just said that but by his face, I could see it was the right answer.

"How about 3 o'clock?" he asked.

That was in 4 hours.

"Ummm okay, my address is 109 Maple Street."

"Great! I will see you then!" he was still smiling.

My legs were shaking. I walked away slowly so as not to give that fact away.

I gripped my bruised and dirty strawberries and headed for the register. Not stopping to get anything else I came there for. I turned around at the last minute and looked back, and he was still standing there. Watching me. And still smiling.

I paid for my strawberries with cash and ran out the door without getting my change.

Chapter 15

I called Betsey as soon as I got in the car, for moral support. She laughed so hard when I told her about the strawberries. "Relax Sarah..." she said to me. Relax? How could I relax in a situation like this? She thought this was the best thing ever. And of course, she would. Betsey always took life in stride; she would never let a little thing like her dead husband coming back from the grave, rattle her nerves. I wished I had an ounce of her ease with this situation.

I had to think, and I had to think fast. T minus 3 hours and counting. I had gotten home and neatened up the house. Although there wasn't much to neaten. I swept the floors and the front porch. Wiped down the bookshelves. I took our wedding photo off its shelf and put it on the foyer table. Then turned it to face the entryway. Then in a moment of self-doubt, I put it back where it went. I didn't want to push too hard, too soon. But then again, I wanted, no I needed him to remember.

I walked into the living room and wondered how I should act. Was this a date? He joked about a date, but I blew that off and offered for him to give an appraisal of the house. Dammit, what was

I thinking? Actually, what *was* I thinking? I felt sick to my stomach. Maybe I shouldn't have invited him over here. Over the course of the next hour, I went back and forth debating inside my head, and sometimes out loud, on whether I had made a huge mistake or a smart move. During all my mental debating, I didn't realize how much time had passed. It was already 2:15 pm.

I ran upstairs to my closet. I was still wearing my t-shirt and shorts from earlier. Should I dress up? If I did, he would certainly know that I changed for him. Was that okay? There's no etiquette or tips for this type of situation. I opted to change. I dug into the very back of my closet. I had several summer dresses to choose from. I put on five before deciding to go back to the first one I had tried on. A green polka dot halter top dress with a slight A-line skirt. I slipped on a pair of white high heeled sandals. I looked at my face. I looked so worn. This last week had taken a lot out of me. I sat down at my vanity table and put on make-up. The vanity table was beautiful, an old Victorian one that Thomas had inherited from his grandmother when she died, it had belonged to her grandmother before her. It was valuable, but its real value was in the memories. When Thomas and I were first married, he would always sit on the bed and watch me in the mirror as I got ready. He would always stare at me dreamily and say, "My god Sarah, you are beautiful..." I never felt as beautiful as I did when I was with him. I put on mascara and lipstick. Not too much. Just enough to accent my features. I looked at my aging face and wondered about Botox and the cosmetic fillers I had seen advertised. Betsey was always getting them these days. She called it "preserving her youth." She urged me to try it. I never had a reason. Until now.

Lastly, I grabbed my old bottle of Giorgio Armani perfume, Thomas' favorite. I had not worn it but once since he died.

The night I wore it, was for an art gallery opening. The gallery was owned by one of my neighbors, Sal Johnston. It was during the first year we lived here. Betsey begged me to go and to take her. She was on the manhunt. Betsey was not the kind of girl who liked to be alone. After she settled into her apartment here in Wilmington, she started mingling immediately. She would find her a man eventually. Betsey was not what you would call gorgeous, yet she always had a profound effect on men. She had jet black hair and hazel eyes. Porcelain white skin. Always kept her hair in a pixie cut. She was one of those women who wear it well. She was a ballerina when she was younger. She no longer had that physique, but she still portrayed sexy better than most. I didn't want to hold her back from life and fun, even though I knew it was most likely a ruse to get me out and active. So, I went with her to the opening. As soon as I sprayed on the perfume, I started to immediately regret the whole night before it had even begun. I spent the entire evening miserable and couldn't wait to get home to get that smell off me. The smell of painful memories, now that I was living a life without Thomas.

I wondered if I should wear the perfume today? And decided against it. I didn't want to jinx myself. Instead, I grabbed my Chanel Blue and put a dab on my wrist and then some behind my ears, just in case. I felt myself blushing again.

2:58 pm. I was pacing, and by pacing, I mean, wearing a path from the front door to the living room window, where I kept repeatedly peeking out. Thomas was never late for anything, so I knew he would be pulling in any second.

I was so nervous; I started to perspire. I turned on the air conditioning. I had not yet run it this year, the spring had been mild, but I could not be covered in sweat when he got here.

3:05 pm. What if he's standing me up?

Then I thought about that smile.

No, he's coming.

3:10 pm I was starting to get distressed.

Maybe he wasn't coming after all.

Just then I saw a car driving slowly up the street, and it was him. I knew it before he even turned on his signal. He pulled into the driveway, and I had to resist the urge to run out the door straight into his arms.

Game face.

The doorbell rang. I walked as slowly as I could muster and opened the door. And there he was. Standing at the front door and he was smiling.

"I guess you found the house okay?" I said smiling back. But I was so nervous; my hands were shaking.

"Yes, it was easy to get here. But I am sorry about being late. I got caught in traffic over on College Street. You know how the traffic can be this time of year. I wanted to call you and let you know, but then I realized I didn't have your number." He seemed a little embarrassed.

"Oh yes, I'm sorry. I should've given it to you."

He stood there in the open door, staring at me. I realized I had not invited him in.

"Do you want to take a look around the house?" I asked him.

"Oh, oh yeah.... I forgot that's why I was coming over," he chuckled.

Why was he laughing about that? I wondered. What did he think he was coming over for? I wasn't the type of girl who just invited strange men over. But of course, he wasn't just some guy....

"Let me run out to my car, and grab a clipboard for notes," he turned and walked back out to the driveway.

I instantly felt guilty for bringing him over here under false pretenses. But now I had no choice but to follow through with it.

He came back in, still smiling. Why was he smiling so much?

"So, where do you want to start?" Every time he spoke to me, he looked directly into my eyes. It made me feel self-conscious.

I motioned around with no real direction.

We went over basic details about the house. Square footage, bedrooms, bathrooms, yard, etc.

I felt irritated. Why didn't he remember any of this?

Then we walked around the downstairs rooms, while he made notes. He paused in the kitchen and looked at me. He was acting like he might say something but never did. He just kept on with questions and writing notes.

We started up the stairs, and step 6 creaked on cue. He stopped and looked at me.

"Looks like somebody needs to get that fixed for you." And he winked.

Why did he wink? Did he remember?

"If I had my tools with me, I would do that right now. But, maybe the next time I'm here, I can do it? That is if you let me come back?"

And there was that smile again. We were still standing on the stairs. I didn't know what to say. I did want him to come back. We went through the rest of the upstairs. He walked past the old vanity without a spark of recognition. Then we went out the back door, and he made some notes about the storage building and the swimming pool. Once he was done, we walked around front, and he put his clipboard in his car. He had a Black BMW sedan three series. Thomas was never into luxury vehicles. Always said they were a waste of money. But he had one now....

I was going to say something to him, and my blood ran cold. I couldn't remember what he said his name was. All I knew was Thomas. I couldn't call him Thomas again, and scare him off. I was scrambling trying to remember what his business card said. Then miraculously I saw a name tag laying on the seat as if placed there for me. Collin Young. Thank god. He closed his car door and looked at me.

"Well, we're all done with that now." And there was that smile again. "Guess I should be going."

Which was actually phrased like a question instead of a statement. My heart began beating so fast that I thought I would drop right there in the driveway.

"Do you want to come in for a while?" I felt my cheeks burning.... again.

"I'd love to Sarah!" well, at least he remembered my name.

We went inside, and I asked him if he would like a drink. He did, so I opened a bottle of California Red wine. We sat out on the back deck and talked. He told me of his days surfing in California and why he enjoyed selling Real Estate.

I told him about my flower garden and how I loved living in Wilmington. Neither of us spoke of our childhoods or the distant past.

I told him about the boys and how proud I was of both of them. I thought I saw him start to tear up but I couldn't tell if he actually was, or if it was wishful thinking? I could not trust my own judgment. He said he didn't have children and wasn't married. He looked genuinely remorseful over that.

I felt sad for him. And for the first time since I saw him a week ago, I started to doubt myself. Was this Thomas after all? I didn't know, but there were so many things about him that were so much like my Thomas. But other things were not like Thomas at all. I still couldn't give up the notion that it was him. I couldn't. I wouldn't.

We finished the bottle about the time the sun was going down.

He looked over at me. "Sarah, you are breathtaking in this light."

"Thank you," I smiled.

It had been a long time since I had acknowledged a genuine compliment from a man.

"I guess I should be going, that is, unless you want to join me for dinner?" he stood up and waited expectantly.

I was starving. For the first time in a very long time, I felt like I could eat a full meal.

"I would love to. Let me just grab a sweater, just in case it's chilly this evening." I answered, trying not to sound too excited.

We walked back inside, and I ran upstairs to grab my purse and a cardigan. I slipped on my heels that I had left by the back door, and we went out and got in his car. His station was set to 103.3 The Hits station. Strange. Thomas didn't like new music. He had only listened to the classics. The Eagles, Bob Seger, Creedence Clearwater Revival, and the like.

"What are you in the mood to eat?" he asked me, as he turned onto Oleander Drive.

"I love Mexican food!" I volunteered.

He looked amused. "I was hoping you'd say that!"

Thomas and I always ate Mexican on our date nights. It was something we both loved. The food, the culture, the music. That's why we had chosen Cancun, Mexico for our special trip. With that thought, I felt anguish rise up from the pit of my soul. And then I looked over at Collin. The same jawline and nose.... the same hearty laugh. And I smiled.

Over dinner, we made small talk about the food and how *sweet* tea doesn't exist anywhere but in the south. Then a look came over Collin's face that I couldn't discern.

"So, tell me about Thomas," he said softly.

I laughed nervously. Tell you about Thomas? Was he kidding? He wasn't. He was still looking at me and he his eyes seemed so sad. Was he trying to remember? Or was he thinking he would never measure up? I looked into those beautiful blue eyes and thought maybe there was a chance still left for me in this world.

"Thomas was the best man I ever knew. And he loved me and our boys like no other. He was my best friend, my lover, my confidant."

"How did he die?" he asked me gently.

"He drowned." I felt a tear run down my face.

He reached across the table and put his hand on mine. I had been nervously shredding a napkin. His hand felt good there and instantly calmed me.

"I'm so sorry, Sarah. I can't imagine how painful that must've been for you. You are an amazing woman, to go through all you have, and come out the other side, so strong."

"Who said I'm strong?" I gave a half laugh.

"You definitely are. If you weren't, you would not be sitting here across from me today." He looked so intently at me.

He paid the check, and we drove back to the house silently. When we pulled into the driveway, he ran around and opened my car door. Something Thomas never did. I got out and started up the walkway. He touched my arm and gently pulled me back. He looked into my eyes.

"Sarah, I know I can't even begin to replace Thomas, but there's something about you that stirs something inside of me. Ever since the day I saw you, I haven't been able to get you off my mind. I hope you will give me a chance to spend some time with you."

I just looked back at him. I didn't know what to say. He pulled me closer and kissed me. A long, deep kiss. My entire body went numb with electricity. And I kissed him back. I felt like a teenager again. Not wanting the kiss to end. Then he stepped back from me.

"I have to go now. If I keep kissing you like that, I won't be able to stay a gentleman."

I took a half step closer, secretly hoping he would break the code of honor.

"Can I have your number now?" He chuckled and then smiled so sweetly at me, I thought I would melt.

I gave him the number, and he entered it into his phone.

"Thank you, Sarah. I had a wonderful time today. I'll call you soon."

He walked me to the front door, and gently kissed my cheek.

"Goodnight, Sarah," he said as he started down the front steps. Then he stopped to look back at me.

"Goodnight Thom...Collin." I couldn't believe I almost just said Thomas again.

He turned and started walking away and then turned and looked back at me again, saying nothing. He got into his car, gave me a quick wave, and drove away.

I stood on the front porch and stared after his taillights until they were out of sight. I walked over and sat on my front porch swing. I listened to the crickets chirping and thought about Collin. I began to cry. I wasn't sure if I was sad or if I was happy. All I knew is that my life had completely changed.

Chapter 16

I was dreaming of Thomas again. He was yelling for help and thrashing around in a deep and wide body of water. It was dark. No moon. I watched from a small boat, and I was sobbing, too afraid to jump in and help him. But then, suddenly, in a last-minute moment of panic, I jump into the water. I swam over to where he was and searched for him, and he's gone. I am looking, and there's nothing but water and darkness. I start crying out his name into the darkness. I started to panic. I am screaming, and then I went under the ebony water. When I woke up, I was shaking from head to toe.

This dream was like many dreams I had been having lately. Night after night. I was exhausted from the disrupted sleep making me sleep in a little later than usual.

I rolled over and checked my phone. 8:45 am. There's a text message from a number I don't recognize.

The message read: "Going to New Bern for a showing. Would love some company."

It took a second for my groggy mind to realize it must be Collin. I sat up immediately and saved his number. He had texted me 45 minutes ago. I was panicked. I didn't want him to think I was ignoring him!

My quick response was not thought out.

"Sure."

I wish I had said more. A one-word response? What was wrong with me?! But it was too late; I had already sent it.

His response was so immediate that it startled me.

"Can I pick you up in 30 minutes?"

I texted back, "Yes, sounds great." There was no way; I was going to say no!

But, 30 minutes? How would I ever pull this off!?

I grabbed a pair of white crop linen pants, and a tan silk v neck blouse, pairing it with a pair of flat sandals and pearls. I pulled my hair into a short ponytail and quickly put on makeup. I looked at myself in the mirror for a long moment wondering what Thomas thought of me now.... I mean Collin thinks of me......God.... I couldn't keep the two straight in my head. They were one and the same to me. But I knew if I had any chance at all with Collin, I would have to leave Thomas out of it for now. I didn't know if I could, but I would try.

I made a cup of coffee to go, pouring it into a clear Tervis mug with a lid. I was sitting in a rocking chair on the front porch when he pulled up. The sun was shining. It was a beautiful morning. I walked out to his car and got inside. I smiled at him. He was even more handsome than I remembered.

"Well, Good Morning, Beautiful!" his eyes sparkled even bluer than I remembered.

Good morning beautiful? That was Thomas' line.

We drove along highway 17 and talked about the beautiful landscape of North Carolina. The tall pines swaying in the wind. The marsh grasses and wildlife. The temperate weather.

We arrived in New Bern about 11:15 am. We drove down Main Street and pulled into the driveway of a white Antebellum style home with huge two-story columns. Saying it was magnificent, was an understatement. He was meeting a couple from Raleigh here at 11:30 am. We walked around the property, as I admired the lush yard. Large Hydrangea bushes filled with giant purple blooms. Daffodils in every mulch bed. A giant magnolia tree's blooms filled the air with luscious perfume. For a moment, I wished I was the one buying this house. A large silver SUV pulled up, and a distinguished couple emerged. Collin met them at their car. I meandered off, so as not to interfere. Collin was so professional and knowledgeable. Even I was impressed.

The showing took about 45 minutes. I was waiting in Collin's car when they emerged from the house. The man shook Collin's hand, and the wife waved to him, as they got into the SUV and drove away.

Collin locked up the house and got back in the car.

"How did it go?" I asked.

"They're going to talk about it, but I think they loved it!" He had a look of accomplishment on his face.

"I loved it; I don't know how they couldn't have!" I truly meant that. It was a magnificent property.

Collin started the car and turned toward me.

"How hungry are you? If you can make it until we get back to the Wilmington area, I'd love to take you somewhere special for lunch." My stomach was rumbling quite a bit, but instead, I said: "Sure, I can make it until we get there." I was curious to see what he had in mind.

We didn't talk much on the drive back. It was a comfortable silence though. I didn't feel like I needed to fill the space with conversation. I just enjoyed being here in the car with him.

We drove through Wilmington and took Highway 133 into Belville. I had never been there before. As we got off of the highway, we rolled down the windows, and the fresh spring air filled the car. I sighed.

He turned down a dirt road and drove slowly down it for a few minutes until a small white two-story home came into view. It had a massive wrap around porch, and it sat just on the river bank.

"It doesn't look open for business," I said humorously, as I got out.

"Nope, they don't get many customers out this way." he laughed

"I guess you figured out by now, that this is my house. I bought it a few months ago."

"It's really beautiful, Collin!" I smiled in appreciation of his taste. I walked around the front yard. Large pecan trees surrounded the place. There were large pink Azalea bushes in front of the house. They were in full bloom. Collin picked one and handed it to me. I held it in my hand. I was giddy.

"So, are you ready to eat?" He smiled and headed up the steps onto the front porch.

"Yes, I'm famished." I followed him inside the house.

We went in through the front door. The entranceway had a staircase to the right side of it and a large framed opening on each side. One leading into the kitchen and the other into a living room with a large fireplace. The house had original hardwood flooring and thick mouldings.

It smelled like an old house, a house filled with years of dust and memories. I loved it.

Collin led me into a 1950's style kitchen. Small and quaint. He opened the door on his stainless-steel refrigerator, which seemed completely out of place in this kitchen.

"You want a beer?"

I looked at my watch. 3pm. I remember the old adage, never drink before 4 pm and laughed under my breath.

"I'd love one, actually."

He grabbed a beer for each of us and led me out to the back porch. There were a small patio table and four chairs. I sat down facing the view of the river. The view was spectacular. His large yard ran down straight to the bank of the river which was lined with trees. But there were enough gaps that you could still see flowing water.

"I'll be right back with lunch. Pimento cheese sandwiches okay? It's real gourmet eating!" He laughed and winked at me.

"That sounds great!" I replied enthusiastically. I could've eaten anything at this point. But I did love pimento cheese, especially the southern variety with a hint of spice.

He reappeared quickly with two plates in hand. He had made sandwiches for both of us. They were cut into triangle halves. There were chips and a pickle on the side.

We ate together, drinking our beers, watching the birds around a bird feeder and squirrels scampering about his yard.

I gasped when a cardinal landed on the railing next to me.

"You know that when you see a cardinal, it means good luck, right?" he offered with a spark in his eyes.

I nodded in response. I looked carefully at his face. His hair was greying, and he had fine lines around his eyes and on his forehead. He was so sexy. How is it fair that men get better with age and we women have to fight and claw to hold onto our youth? I wondered if he noticed the same wear and tear on me? I suddenly felt very self-conscious.

He smiled gently at me. "You are a very beautiful woman, Sarah."

Could he read my mind?

He reached across the table, and touched my face with his thumb and ran it across my cheek.

Then he pushed a stray hair from my face.

"Truly beautiful," he said in almost husky voice.

I stood up nervously. I wasn't ready for this.

"Could we walk down to the river?" I asked as a diversion

"Of course, we can. I was thinking of doing some fishing if you want to join me?"

We cleaned up the lunch dishes, and he ran upstairs to change clothes.

I walked through the kitchen into a small dining room. There was a buffet table in there with some photos on top. They were of Collin surfing, fishing, and mountain climbing. He looked so handsome.

He came into the room, and he wasn't wearing a shirt, just some black swimming trunks. His body was tan and sculpted. My whole body tingled. He looked amazing for his age. Hell, he looked amazing for any age. I looked down. Embarrassed, and still wondering if he could read my thoughts.

We headed down to the bank of the river. He had a wooden dock that extended out into the water.

We walked down to the end of the dock, and he bent over and pulled on a rope that went down into the water. His back muscles flexed as he pulled a crabbing basket up. It was empty.

He walked back up the pier to a little woodshed that sat on the banks next to the pier. He pulled out two fishing rods and a tackle box.

"So, do you want to fish with me?" he asked sheepishly as if he already knew the answer.

"No, I'll just watch," I smiled.

We sat down at the end of the pier together, and he cast his line into the flowing water.

Once again, we sat in comfortable silence. The river was bubbling, and birds were singing. There was the occasional unknown splash from somewhere on the river. A natural symphony. I looked at him as sat quietly with his rod in hand. The attraction I had to him was overwhelming me. I looked at his hands, and my thoughts went to imagining them on me, and I looked at his mouth and pictured his tongue running down my neck. That made me tingle, and I felt faint. He looked over at me and smiled. He put his hand on mine and intertwined his fingers with mine. We sat like that for a while, neither of us moving. We watched a family of ducks swim by us. The yellow ducklings were so fuzzy and cute. A fish pulled his bobber down, and he reeled in a tiny striped bass. We both laughed.

He hauled in a couple of bigger Bass and put them on a stringer that he left hanging in the water.

Then the light began to change, and the breeze got a little cooler. I shivered.

He put the rods away and brought the fish back up to the house.

"So, you want to stay for dinner?" he asked with a satisfied smile.

"Let me guess...fish?" I laughed.

"Yep, grilled right here on my back porch. The best in the south!" he beamed.

I volunteered to go inside and make something for us to eat on the side. I went into his kitchen and looked through the cabinets finding some rice and lemons. He also had a bag of asparagus in the freezer. Not bad for a bachelor. I had actually expected to find maybe a frozen pizza and some chips at the most.

I made the rice and squirted the fresh lemon over it. The asparagus, I steamed with a little salt and a dash of lemon as well. He came inside just as I was finishing up.

He grabbed two more beers and some plates and forks.

We ate outside as the sun was going down. The light over the river was spectacular.

Once the mosquitos started to bite, we headed inside.

I did the dishes, and he went into the living room and put on some music. After I was finished cleaning up the kitchen, I joined him in there. I slipped off my shoes and walked with bare feet across the room. There was a fire going in the fireplace, and I could hear the distinct voice of Frank Sinatra coming from an old record player.

"Can you believe this player and a bunch of records were left here when I bought the house?" he said triumphantly.

He was sitting on the large brick hearth by the fire. I went over and sat down beside him. He turned his body toward me.

"This has been the best day I have had in a very long time." His eyes glistened in the firelight.

"Me too," I replied quietly

He put his hand behind my neck and pulled me toward him.

He put his mouth on mine and kissed me slowly and deliberately. I kissed him back. My body was responding to his every move.

Then he stood up and took my hand. He led me upstairs to his bedroom. He turned on a small lamp beside the bed.

I stood in the doorway. He walked over to me and kissed my lips softly. Then he reached up and unbuttoned the button on the back of my blouse, and then he gently pulled it over my head. He then unfastened my pants and slipped them off. I pulled my hair out of the ponytail and let it fall around my face.

He looked at me and whispered, "You are so beautiful."

I knew he meant it.

He unhooked my bra and pulled off my panties and let them slip to the floor. He led me over to the bed and told me to lay down. I did, and he came and propped himself up beside me. I lay there beside him. He looked at me with such tenderness. He ran his hands slowly and deliberately over my entire body, feeling every curve and crevice. I noticed he was trembling. I grabbed his face and kissed him. Passion consumed me. There was no Thomas, only Collin, right there in the moment. He rolled over on top of me, and my hands ran down his well-defined back. He kissed my neck, my face, and my lips. And when he finally put himself inside me, I gasped with pleasure. It felt so right to be with him like this. When we were finished, he wrapped the top blanket around himself and got up. He turned around and looked at me, as I lay still naked on his bed.

"You are an amazing woman, Sarah."

He disappeared into the bathroom with the blanket and all. I laid there wondering, how could I could have forgotten Thomas so easily?

I got dressed, and after he came out of the bathroom, he asked me to stay the night. But I needed to go home.

As he drove me back home, my thoughts went back to all the passionate nights I had with Thomas, and I felt a sense of guilt. But why? I didn't even know. I couldn't make sense of my own thoughts. Collin reached over and put his hand on mine. I was feeling something growing inside of me that I could not quite understand. I was so confused. I wanted Collin. But was it for Collin, or was it for Thomas? I didn't know, and quite honestly, I had stopped caring who he was. I was content here in this place of limbo. Caught in between two worlds. Lost and found at the same time. And I was happier than I could remember being in a long time.

Chapter 17

—⟨∞⟩—

Adam sat at his desk at the Social Services office tapping a pencil on his desk absentmindedly. He was pondering his mother's strange behavior and Emily's upcoming birthday.

I want to do something really special for Emily. The plans were to take her to the planetarium near Ocean Isle and then maybe on a sunset cruise. Something really romantic. But Emily had grown a little distant lately. The only conclusion I could come to was that she was mad that I hadn't introduced her to my mom yet. And it was complicated by the fact that Mom was still acting strangely, and it had been going on for weeks now. She was never there when I went to do anything at the house lately. Something was definitely going on. And I had barely heard from her when before she had texted or called me every day without fail.

I picked up my desk phone and started to dial Mom's cell when my cell phone dinged. It was Emily.

Her text read: "I do love you, Adam."

There was an energy to that text that made me very nervous. Yeah, I would have to do something about this and soon. I dialed the home phone and was shocked when mom answered right away.

"Hi, Mom."

"How are you, sweetheart?" She acted as if nothing was out of the ordinary.

"I'm sorry I missed you the last few times you've been here, I was out running errands," she said aloofly.

How many errands can one woman run? I wondered.

"Mom, there's something I need to tell you......"

I was met with dead silence.

"I've met someone, Mom. And she's amazing."

There was more silence, and I felt my pulse rising. I was getting angry. How could she be so selfish?

"Her name is Emily, and I really want you to meet her." I know my voice had a desperate tone.

Then came the shock of a lifetime, Mom wasn't mad at all, in fact, she sounded happy.

"Adam, I think that is wonderful! I'm so happy for you! And yes, please do bring her over. What about tomorrow night?" she sounded genuinely enthusiastic.

I was completely dumbfounded. All the stress, anger, and worry...for nothing.

"Let me ask Emily to be sure, but I think tomorrow would work for her."

I hung up the phone with a great sense of relief.

I texted Emily right away. "I hope you don't have plans for tomorrow night because we have a dinner date with my mom" I followed it with a smiling emoji.

She texted back two thumbs up. Her reply was less than enthusiastic.

I started thinking that maybe I should go over, and hang out with Mom some tonight. That way I could tell her a little more about Emily to ensure things, would, in fact, go well tomorrow night. That is if Mom was even home.

The rest of the day was filled with phone calls. They had me fielding the incoming calls for Child Protection Services. Some days it was really draining dealing with calls about people not taking care of their kids. The worst ones were the calls about kids being hurt. Those brought out a side of me that I didn't know I had before this job. I seriously wanted to hurt them for laying a hand on a child. And I wanted to make damn sure they could never hurt a child again. But our job here was to protect the children, and that's what I tried to focus on. Helping the innocents. That's what kept me going. It also sparked a new interest in Child Psychology. Maybe a switch in Specialty might be in order.

I left work right at 5:00 pm. Summer had hit, and the tourists were back making the traffic on College Road worse than usual. I grudgingly headed back to my apartment to feed the cat. Emily had asked me to watch her cat this week while her apartment was being repainted. The cat was a fat grey Persian named Sasha, and it was the laziest creature I had ever seen. I wasn't fond of cats, but this one was semi-tolerable. Mostly because Emily loved the thing so much. Though dealing with cat hair on everything was not a joy. I had to pick the cat hair off my food before I could eat it. I had to lint roll my clothes every day before putting them on. Somehow the cat hair made it into my closet and onto hanging clothes. And its food, the smell makes me gag every time I open a can of Kitty Delight and oh yes, let's not forget the litter box. Where the thing produces a shit, the size of a small cucumber and I am expected to take a little shovel and scoop it out for her majesty Queen Sasha. I started to realized maybe I wasn't as tolerant of the cat as I had previously thought.

I stepped inside the front door and instantly smelled the smell coming from the litter box.

"What the hell died inside of you!?" I yelled to Sasha, as she sat on the top of the couch staring at me. She had that stupid smug cat look while depositing ungodly cat hair onto my suede leather couch.

I scooped the excrement out and put it inside a scented baggie. Who doesn't love the smell of shit and vanilla? Then I went into the kitchen to feed the thing and called out to her.

"Here kitty kitty, dumbass kitty."

Sasha slowly pranced into the kitchen. I opened up the new can of food which didn't smell much better than the litter box and threw the open can on the floor. Emily had this white porcelain dish with paw prints all over it to feed her in. But it had to be washed each time she ate, so I opted for the easier route. Shit food Al la can.

I went into my bedroom and switched into jeans and a Sea Hawks t-shirt. I looked in the mirror. The beard I was growing was coming in nicely. Not like the patchwork beard I have seen on a lot of the guys my age. I put my hands on my face and rubbed it. I could not help but smile. I could not help but be pleased with myself. The beard made me feel more manly. And in my line of work, a beard was appropriate, maybe even expected. When I become Dr. Avery, it will suit me even more.

I shut the apartment door and locked it. I got into my blue Volkswagen Passat and drove toward Mom's house. It wasn't quite 6:00 pm, and I knew that Mom didn't eat much when she wasn't cooking for me, so I decided to stop in at Telly's Burger & Grill. I picked up some food for us.

I drove down the street my mom lives on listening to Bob Seger's Night Moves on the radio, and as I got closer, I saw mom's car was there, but also a car I had never seen before was sitting in the driveway. A black BMW sedan. I unconsciously stiffened my jaw. I didn't like this at all.

I walked in the front door and could faintly hear music playing from the backyard. I passed through the kitchen and set the bag of food on the table and walked to the French doors that led out to the back deck and peered out the glass window pane. I could see Mom. She was laughing and talking to someone. A man. All I could see was the back of his head. The man leaned in toward Mom and started kissing her. Before I realized what I was doing, I busted out the door, and I was yelling.

"Who the hell are you?!" I was looking directly at the imposter's back.

Mom headed straight for me. Her face was white as a ghost.

"Adam, what a surprise!"

"I didn't know you were coming over today." She stammered

The man turned around and looked straight at me. I felt rage in the pit of my soul, and I almost growled.

"Who the hell is he, Mom!?"

Her face went from white to red.

"His name is Collin Young, and he's a friend of mine." She looked utterly defiant with her hands on her hips.

"Well, none of my *friends* stick their tongues down my throat!" I felt the words glide out of my mouth, but I was too angry to sensor them.

Then the man approached me. There was something semi-familiar about him, but I just couldn't place it. My body stiffened in reaction as the man reached out his hand to shake mine.

I kept my hands firmly by my side and then crossed my arms to make sure he got the message.

"You must be Adam," the man said. He didn't look angry or put off by my behavior.

"I'm Collin." He smiled.

"I'm sorry that my being here upset you, I'll just go ahead and leave now, to let you and your mom have some time to talk."

Mom put her hand on his arm. "You don't have to go, Collin!" she glared over at me.

"I think it would be better for you and Adam to spend some time together now."

He leaned over and kissed her cheek. "I'll call you tomorrow."

Her face beamed as she looked up at him and I instantly felt ashamed at my outburst.

I mustered up the right words.

"Hey look, I'm sorry about yelling, you really caught me off guard." That was the best I could muster for him.

Collin walked over and patted me on the shoulder.

"Don't you worry about it, it's good that she has such a protective son."

Mom followed him out to the front door, and after a few minutes, she came back to where I was standing in the backyard. I hadn't moved a muscle.

"Well?" I asked her.

"First of all, must I remind you that I am a grown woman? I can have a man friend over, and kiss him all I like if that's what I want to do." she looked utterly intractable.

"Yeah, but you don't have *man friends.*" I looked at her questioningly.

"Well I do now!" she said with an irritated tone.

And if I didn't know better, I would've certainly thought she was mad that I ran him off.

I went inside and got the food I brought her. She took the hamburger and fries and wolfed them down like a starved animal. I just stared at her in disbelief. So much for her lack of appetite.

"Well, you seem to have quite an appetite there, Mom." My mouth was hanging open in such disbelief that I could not even eat my own food.

She giggled as she stuffed fries in her mouth. Did she seriously just giggle?

She wiped her mouth with a napkin and then sat back in her chair looking intently at me. Like she was waiting for something.

"Where did you meet this guy?" I inquired.

She leaned in close and smiled an eerie smile. "So..did he seem familiar at all to you?"

"No, he didn't." I lied.

"Did you get a good look at him?" she pressed

"Yes, he just looks like some guy who was kissing my mom." I glared at her.

"Well, he's not just some guy Adam..." she paused

"I actually think he might be your father." Holy shit, did she just say that he was Dad? And the scariest part of all was that she looked dead serious.

I looked at her face, and I instantly felt like I was going to throw up.

"What did you just say!?" I felt the anger and fear welling up inside of me.

"I know it sounds crazy, but I think somehow that he is your dad, Adam. I don't know how or why, but somehow some way the universe has seen fit to return him to me." Tears slid down her face.

I stood up. I was enraged.

"Oh my god, mom, he is not Dad!" My heart was in my throat. I could have her committed right now for this. I wouldn't, I couldn't, but there was just cause.

She looked completely downtrodden. What did she expect me to say? Dammit!

"Mom, I'm sorry, but you're just confused. You clearly have feelings for this man, okay, I get that. But you can't really believe that he's Dad. Dad has been dead for 14 years, and he's never coming back!"

I felt my voice rising with intensity. My own pain was rising to the surface.

"Did he say something to you to make you believe that he was Dad?"

I felt maybe he was a con man after my mom's money.

"No, he denies being Thomas. And I'm not even sure myself, but there are just things about him..." her voice trailed off.

"Has he asked you about your finances?" I kept pushing.

Her face immediately turned bright red with anger.

"NO ADAM, HE'S A GOOD MAN, AND I THINK I AM IN LOVE WITH HIM, SO DON'T YOU DARE DISRESPECT HIM!" she yelled so loud that I'm sure the neighbors heard her.

I was actually startled that she had screamed at me.

"Mom, for crying out loud, just calm down already! I am just worried about you."

I stepped toward her and touched her arm.

Her face instantly softened, and her body relaxed.

"Adam, I know you are worried, but you need to trust me."

"I do, mom." I lied.

There was no way I trusted her now. She thinks some guy she has just met, that maybe looks a little like Dad, to actually be him come back from the dead. I was scared. She needed help. Serious help.

We sat back down, and she talked on and on to me, about Collin, and things they had been doing together. She told me about his house in Belville, and the dock there. When the heck had she been to his house? This explained all her absences and aloofness of late.

She told me of the dates they had been on and how much fun she had with him. I was happy to see her so happy. She talked on like a school girl. Why did girls always act this way about new relationships? But I was seriously worried about this situation.

She seemed lucid and had a firm grasp on the reality of everything except for the part where she thought Collin could be Dad. I felt that maybe, she was simply feeling guilty over this new relationship, and transferred her emotions to justify the feelings. That's why she's mixed up. That was the diagnosis I would stick with. For now......

I never got around to talking to her about Emily. She went on the whole night gushing about Collin. And all I could think of was beating in his face. Before I left, I reminded her that Emily and I would be coming to dinner tomorrow. I asked if Collin would be here and prayed she would say no. She did.

"I can't wait to meet her." she smiled genuinely and hugged me.

"I am so happy for you, Adam!"

We walked out to the car together.

"I'm sorry I yelled at your b-boyfriend..." The words got stuck in my mouth.

I couldn't believe my mom had a boyfriend. I wanted to kill him, literally drag him out in the street and kick his teeth in, for putting his mouth on her. I quaked at the thought of the others things he might have done to her. She's so naïve! Killing him seemed like the best choice. But she was smiling. Genuinely smiling. Something I hadn't seen in 14 years. So, I'd have to let him live. For the time being.

I hugged Mom and drove home. On the drive, my mind raced, all I could think about was that man kissing her, and I wanted to vomit. She had not dated before, and I wasn't used to it. I didn't like this one bit. I realized this was most likely some kind of Freudian response, but it didn't stop the way I felt. All I wanted to do now was get home and get into my bed. Forget this whole shitty day.

I drove into to my apartment complex parking lot. College kids were at the pool, having a party, drinking, laughing, and screaming. Now that I was in graduate school, I felt myself elevated above these silly college kids, so I scoffed at their behavior. Even though, just last year, I would have been out there with them. I found a parking spot and walked up to my apartment, and when I got up there, I saw the lights were on. Did I leave the lights on? I opened the door and went inside. In the kitchen stood Emily holding an empty can of cat food in her hand. The look on her face was one I had never seen before. I winced because I knew I was in trouble.

Chapter 18

*I*t was a beautiful early summer morning. I drove my car out to the beach to go for a walk. This was something that had been part of my routine before I met Collin. I enjoyed the serenity of the early mornings on the Carolina shoreline. The salt spray misted in the air and smelled glorious. The sun was just rising and the lighting was spectacular. Most of the tourists were still tucked in their beds dreaming of sand, sun, and laughter. And I had the beach to myself. The waves crashing and occasional seagull calling soothed me in a way that I couldn't explain. I slipped off my shoes and left them at the wooden boardwalk that led down to the beach. Walking along the edge, the water tickled my toes, still a little cold from winter. The long-legged avocets ran ahead in the tides searching for breakfast. I started thinking of the last few months with Collin and how wonderful it had been. He fit inside of my heart neatly. Like Thomas somehow had left just enough space for him in there.

We had so much fun together. We had been bowling, kayaking, and even rented jet skis. We played like children. I laughed so much with him. More than I could remember laughing with anyone. Even with Thomas. He was so funny and adventurous. He wanted to live every moment like there was no tomorrow. To pull every good thing from each day that he possibly could. He had an appreciation for life that you rarely see and it was contagious. Now he was talking of us taking Sailing lessons and learning to Shag to Beach Music. Being with Collin made me feel young again. Alive. And so beautiful. Sometimes he would just stare at me, and I would look over at him and then he would say all these cliché things about my beauty. But strangely, I believed him. It was something in his eyes. Something that told me he was speaking from his heart.

Our relationship was taking on a natural flow. We had started meeting each other's friends. A few weeks ago, I took him to a cookout at Betsey's house. Betsey kept coming over and whispering in my ear about the uncanny resemblance between Collin and Thomas but then quickly followed it up saying that of course there was no way it was Thomas. And how apparently my taste in men was just that great. And definitely consistent. I couldn't help but wonder if she wanted to say more but didn't dare to, for fear of encouraging me in my delusions. Instead, she chose to question me about the sex. Betsey was never one to hold back. She was forthright and open. That was one of the things I loved so much about her. I told her it was pretty great and she was thrilled for me. Saying it was about time! We both laughed. It was true. We sat, sipping wine, and watched our guys standing by her pool drinking beer and talking. Collin and Jack were getting along great. Which was a relief to both Betsey and me. We were hoping that they would hit it off so we could all hang out together more. I watched Collin standing there, tall and tan in his white Polo and blue seersucker shorts. Betsey was right he was a beautiful man. Sexy. Just looking at him gave me flutters.

And the sex *was* incredible. I never realized how much I missed sex until being with him. 14 years had passed without a second thought of it, and now I couldn't get enough of him. We had made love on his dock in the dark, right on there on the wood planks, just last night. With the moonlight overhead, he had kissed me all over. He was always so gentle and giving. I shivered with delight at the memory.

My feelings for Collin were strong but I still couldn't shake the similarities between him and Thomas. But there were differences too. Most days I accepted the *not knowing* gracefully, and just enjoyed our time together. However, on days like today, my mind was my biggest tormentor. Racing with thoughts and questions that couldn't or wouldn't be answered. I learned how to silence them. But I had decided I had had enough of this mental torture. I could not go on living in limbo, caught in between two worlds. And I was thankful, so very grateful for Collin. Despite the mixed emotions and thoughts about him and Thomas, I was enjoying the love and happiness he had brought into my life. But now today, I was ready to embrace the unknown. Putting behind me, all the doubts and questions, I was ready to move forward and accept my new life and stop questioning it so much. It was the only way I could ever have peace. Looking at him and wondering about the quirks that were so much like Thomas was beginning to hold me back from seeing Collin for who he really was. I was forcing him to live in someone else's shadow. The guilt of that overwhelmed me. If he knew, he would think that I was only with him because of Thomas. And that wasn't it. Maybe that was the initial attraction, but now, it was different. I was different. I didn't know if I could ever shake the suspicions, but I wanted to love Collin, free of restrictions or expectations. To give him all of myself. Without adding Thomas into his every move. I was tired of the incessant comparisons. I was tired of making comparisons like Thomas doesn't like chocolate, while I would watch Collin eat a Hershey bar. It was awful that the man couldn't even eat a candy bar without my scrutiny. Or thinking about how Thomas didn't speak Spanish, while Collin had a conversation in Spanish with a Hispanic mom and her child that we met on a walk one afternoon. He was crouched down talking to the child, and I was judging him. It felt so wrong and I wanted it to stop.

Today I had chosen a different beach than usual to walk. I had driven down to Sunset Beach because I was on a mission. I walked along until I saw what I was looking for. The Kindred Spirit Mailbox. I saw the American Flag flapping and the box sitting there in the sand. The Kindred Spirit box has been here for around 34 years. Attracting thousands to share letters and notes, messages written in the journal left inside. There are messages of hope, sadness, and memories of loved ones. The mailbox was a place to say things you couldn't say anywhere else.

I felt in my pocket and pulled out a letter. A letter to Thomas. I didn't even know why I was putting it in the Kindred Spirit box but the compulsion to do so overwhelmed me. Maybe this box possessed a power to heal, maybe set me free.

I sat down at the foot of the mailbox to re-read what I had written late last night after returning from Collin's. A letter goodbye. I had been angry over not being able to say goodbye to Thomas and a therapist that I saw once had recommended I write such a letter as this one. I was never ready until now. I held the letter in my hand, written on softly edged stationary with a little silver bird stamp at the top. A gift from my mother on my last birthday. It had probably cost her more than $40 for the box of 8. I had never used one of them until now. I opened the envelope and pulled the letter out.

My dearest Thomas,

I wish you were here with me now. Standing beside me so I could tell you all that is in my heart. Writing this letter to you is one of the hardest things I have ever had to do. It's like I'm closing the door on us. Something I know I can never truly do. I am writing you this letter because I have met someone. He reminds me so much of you. The similarities between the two of you are numerous and it causes me not to be able to love him the way I should because I keep wanting and expecting him to be you. But no one can really take your place in my heart. I keep wanting something from him that he cannot give. He's good for me though and I am thankful he is here but I wish you were the one I spent my nights with. My heart yearns for you. To touch your face and kiss your lips. For you are the love of my life.

You always have been and always will be. From the first time I saw your face, my heart became yours. You gave me love in a way I did not know love could exist. I can never thank you enough for the wonderful years that you gave me and for our beautiful boys. I look at them and cannot help but see you inside of them. As they grew, I saw you in their smiles, their laughter, and their creativity. And then now as men, I still see you in them. Adam's kindness and drive to succeed and Blake's intelligence and ingenuity. They have all the best parts of you.

When you left me, part of me went with you. I didn't want to live a life without you. I felt so alone and lost. These last 14 years have been awful without you. I have missed you every second of every single

112

day. And I know I will continue to do so until the day I die. And when I do, I will go straight into eternity, looking for you. For with you is where I belong. Until that time, know that I am yours and always will be.

    All my love,
    Sarah

    My tears dropped onto the letter running the ink on some of the words. I quickly placed the letter back inside the envelope. I stood up and dusted the sand off. I walked over and opened the mailbox. Inside of it was a community journal, and there were also many letters and postcards of all colors and sizes. Letters in children's handwriting and formally written ones. There were letters to loved ones. Letters for The Kindred Spirit Mailbox visitors to read. Letters of encouragement and joy. Notes of sadness and loss too. But the overwhelming feeling of the box left me with a hope that we are not alone that somehow some way we connect and heal together. That this box connects us all in love. I closed it and felt a peace that I hadn't felt since Thomas died.

    I walked back in the direction of the car. By this time there were a few dads out on the beach setting up sun canopies for the day. There were also a few joggers and shell seekers. I walked along smiling because I knew I was meeting Betsey today for lunch. The same place I was headed to when I ran into Collin the very first time. I shook my head at my duality. One minute ago, I was crying over my letter to Thomas and promising my unending love to him and now smiling because I was thinking of Collin. I wasn't sure what to make of it all. I felt guilty and ashamed but so happy at the same time.

I pulled into my driveway and there sat Collin's BMW. I walked in the front door and he was just coming down the steps with a hammer in his hand.

"Hi, there!" I want you to know that I just fixed that squeaky step for you!" He beamed with pride. That smile made my heart pick up its pace immediately.

"So where did you go this morning?" he asked as he came up behind me and wrapped his arms around me and pulled me close.

"I went to the beach..." I tried to say but he started kissing the back of my neck and I stuttered, "to take a walk."

I turned my body around to face him, and he kissed me long and hard. My whole body warmed instantly to his touch, but I pulled back. I had to fight every instinct of wanting him.

"Adam might drop by any minute," I said wanting to feel his mouth on mine again.

"How about some coffee?" I asked trying to sound disinterested in what he was offering.

"As long as you sweeten it with a kiss," he said and winked at me.

His silly one-liners made me swoon with happiness.

I heard a car door slam, and as if on cue Adam walked in the front door.

Adam smiled and said good morning to Collin. He and Collin had made peace with each other over the last few weeks. Emily had somehow softened Adam. He was more accepting of a lot of things these days. We had just had dinner, the four of us, at Sergio's Italian restaurant. Emily was a doll and she really seemed to make Adam happy. I liked her a lot. She was a charismatic girl. Charming and sweet but strong. A good balance. And Very beautiful. She brought out a side of Adam that I had never seen before. Something about her made him more carefree and he

114

smiled a lot more. I was so happy to finally see him happy. He was much freer not carrying the burden of 100% of the responsibility for me and my life any longer. He still came by quite often to check on me and to see if I needed anything. I rarely did. I hired a lawn care company and Collin took care of the minor things like changing light bulbs when he was over.

I think that Adam felt a little dejected in some ways over me not needing him but our relationship was better for it. Sometimes it can be just as disturbing not to be needed as much as it is to be needed too much.

He had coffee with us as he and Collin talked about the new batting cages that they were building in town. They shared a love of baseball. It always gave them something to talk about. Collin pulled for the LA Dodgers and Adam pulled for the Boston Red Sox just like his dad, but baseball was baseball and it helped them connect. They had even gone to a Wilmington Sharks game together. The minor league baseball team here in Wilmington was pretty good and the baseball park was a lot of fun. I was glad to see them becoming friends. I had my doubts for a while but now there wasn't any sign of that hostility from the first time that they met.

After coffee, I left to go downtown. I wanted to do a little shopping before meeting Betsey. I left the guys there at the house, talking and I headed out. My favorite shop downtown was A La Marie, a little boutique that sold locally designer clothing, handmade jewelry and it smelled of the most amazing candles and potpourri. They carried super trendy clothes and shoes. Brands like Golden London and Gigi Monroe. I wanted to pick out a new dress. I hadn't bought anything for myself in a long while. I walked inside and a little bell chimed alerting the attendant I was there. A cold bust of AC and potpourri met me. Never underestimate a little shopping therapy, I thought to myself. It was so peaceful in here. Not like the department stores at the mall with their red tag sales and racks upon racks of clothing. The prices in here were a little higher but well worth the whole shopping experience. After browsing several racks of dresses, I settled on a petal pink dress with an empire waist, scoop neck, and the skirt portion had an overlay of lace. I paired it with a bracelet made of Pink Calcite stones. Calcites were supposed to give clarity of thought and bring closure to open-ended situations, so I thought I'd give it a try. Betsey had told me to try out wearing stones, she always wore a blue Labradorite, that she said was for protection. She truly believed in the power of stones.

I took my choices up to the register and the young girl wearing a floral kimono and a flower in her hair, wrapped my items individually in tissue paper and then placed them in a paper bag with twine handles and their logo beautifully stamped on the outside. And then she tied a beautiful polka dot ribbon onto it. Little touches like that made it all worth it; I thought as I paid my hefty tab. I walked out gratified and excited about what I had chosen. And I couldn't wait to wear it. Collin was taking me to a dinner that was being hosted by his real estate office to benefit The Sea Turtle Rescue and Rehabilitation Center, a local charity here to help save and protect The Sea Turtles of North Carolina. This would be the first time I would be meeting his co-workers. I felt like this was one more step in becoming an official couple.

I met Betsey outside of The Sailfish Restaurant. She was standing there in white cigarette pants and a black dolman top and wearing a pair of Christian Louboutin heels. When she walked the signature, red soles would flash with each step. She always looked fabulous. She oozed glamour from her pores. When she greeted me, she kissed each of my cheeks. A greeting she had always done. "How are you darling?" she laughed as if she already knew the answer.

Betsey and I had a great lunch. We ate sushi and drank Sake. We talked for 2 hours while getting the stink eye from our server for taking up the spot for too long. But the sake made for a relaxing lunch and we were enjoying just being there together.

"Nothing like a nice afternoon buzz!" Betsey said as she ordered a second bottle of Sake.

It looked like I would be driving her home, which I did quite often after our lunch dates. Sometimes I wondered if she was as happy as she always appeared.

She did seem genuinely happy though. Since her divorce, I had yet to hear her complain of one single thing. She embraced life entirely just as it came to her. I wished I had one ounce of her natural freedom. I guess the drinking that she did was just one more way for her to celebrate life. At least I hoped that was it. If anybody in this world deserved happiness, it was Betsey.

That night I sat alone by the cold, empty fireplace and stared into the darkness. I didn't have any lights on except a small lamp on the end table. Collin had a late showing for a house over in Ogden and I needed a night to myself anyway. I was feeling melancholy. I wasn't sure if I was happy about the step being fixed or not. That was my one anchor to Thomas in this house. But maybe it was for the best after all. I was just holding onto ghosts. Out of all these associations I had made of Collin to Thomas, I wondered now how much was being created in my mind to make the pieces fit. I wondered how hurt Collin would be if he knew how much of Thomas I had tied into mine and his relationship. And how he would feel if he knew how much I truly still loved Thomas. But really, I loved them both. There was no separating or distinguishing where my love for Thomas ended and my love for Collin began.

I fell asleep that night and dreamed again of Thomas. But this time I dreamt that Thomas came to me, which he never did in any of my dreams of him. We were standing together high on a mountaintop. The wind was blowing.

He kept saying just the words, *"Let go."*

"Let go."

"Let go."

Why was he saying Let go?

And I screamed, "Of what!?"

And he said it again.

"Let go!"

I screamed, "Thomas, I can't."

He then said, "You have to let go, to be able to hold on."

And then I cried out "I can't! I can only truly love you Thomas, and no one else!"

He then turned away from me, and walked toward the mountain's edge and then stepped right off the cliff and out of sight.

I screamed "NO!" and ran and looked over the edge where he had just stepped off and he was gone. I was looking over the cliff at nothing. Not a sign of him anywhere.

I woke up crying. And immediately I was frustrated and angry. What did that dream mean? Did it mean I didn't love Collin? It couldn't possibly mean that.

And why was I dreaming of Thomas every single night!? It certainly didn't make moving on any easier.

As I stood in the shower that morning, I kept repeating the dream in my mind. Was it my subconscious or could it have been Thomas speaking from beyond the grave? And what did it mean? I was driving myself crazy overanalyzing it. I stood in the shower thinking until the water ran cold, startling me back to reality.

I ate breakfast in silence, still thinking of the dream. Was he responding to my letter? He said to let go. Was it to let go of him, to be able to hold onto Collin? At least I knew he was right about that. But knowing and doing were two different things.

My phone rang soon after breakfast. It was Collin. His voice was a welcome reprise from my torturous thoughts. He invited me on a surprise date over lunch. I was eager to find out what he had planned. It was such a romantic gesture, but that was Collin. He was always doing something romantic.

The distraction of getting ready for the date helped me forget about the dream. Collin didn't give me any idea of what we were doing. All he told me was to dress comfortably and wear a swimsuit underneath.

I had never worn a swimsuit around Collin before and I was nervous. I didn't have the body of a twenty-year-old anymore. My body was still in good shape overall but the firmness of youth had long left my thighs and tummy and I carried a few extra pounds that I didn't ask for. I opted for a backless one piece. It was black and cut high on the thighs. The design was sexy. I looked at myself in the mirror self-consciously and winced. It would have to work. Over it, I threw on a grey and white striped romper and pulled my hair back with a black scarf and large white sunhat. With it, I wore my black Chanel sunglasses.

He picked me up right at 11:30 am and drove to Wrightsville Beach. I immediately thought, the beach? I was a little disillusioned. I didn't know what I had expected, but the beach wasn't it.

He went to the trunk and pulled out a blanket, a bottle of wine, and a picnic basket. I was immediately embarrassed about my attitude. He led me out to a quiet part of the beach, away from the crowds. He spread out the blanket and motioned for me to sit down. He opened the picnic basket and pulled out the feast he had bought for us from Chip's Deli. He had brought two Monaco Sandwiches with Lemon Pepper Chicken and Provolone, Fruit Salad, and a bean salad. And for dessert, he brought Caramel Apple Pie.

It was in fact, the most romantic date I had ever been on. We nibbled on sandwiches and gazed out at the sea. The ease of being together was undeniably perfect. I looked over at him and caught him looking at me. I wondered what he was thinking. I hoped it was about me. By the look in his eyes, I'm sure it was.

He used a radio app on his phone for some musical ambiance. He chose a station that played old jazz. And when Etta James' "At Last," came on, he stood up and reached for my hand. He pulled me close, and we danced together there on the sand. I knew people were watching, and I didn't care. I was so lost in this moment. Of being here with him. He whispered in my ear, "Sarah, I love you more than you can even imagine." Tears immediately came to my eyes. This was the first time he had said out loud to me, what I already knew he was feeling.

"I love you too, Collin." I laid my head on his shoulder. And as we danced there together, I was overwhelmed with love for this man. This man. Who stood here with me in flesh and blood. I was a traitor to my own heart, but I was too far gone to look back.

Chapter 19

❧⟡❧

Fall came discreetly to Wilmington. The only change from Summer was the slight nip at night. The days were still blistering hot. It was a lazy Saturday afternoon, and I sat on the front porch swing of Collin's house rocking back and forth. There was a slight humid breeze blowing. Just enough to cool the sweat that was forming on my face. I was drinking homemade lemonade from lemons I had hand squeezed. I added in agave for sweetness and mint leaves for a touch of extra freshness. I loved the crackling sound it made as I had poured it into an ice filled glass. I sipped the tart sweetness and sighed. Birds were singing and the breeze smelled of fresh cut grass. The swing made a creaking sound as it moved back and forth. I looked up at the deep blue sky trying to decipher shapes in the clouds. Something I had not done since childhood. I felt so free and happy. A distinct feeling of satisfaction seeped into my bones. It had been a long time since I had felt this way.

Suddenly I heard the rumbling of car tires on gravel and I smiled. Collin's car was in sight. He was back. His black car was getting covered with gravel dust as he came down the road.

Something that he did not seem to mind. Collin had left me here two hours ago. He had gone out for a last minute showing of a newly listed house in downtown Wilmington. A historic beauty built in the 1800's and it was registered with the Historical Society. Those homes sold like hotcakes and for a mint of a price. With one sale, he would be set financially for the year.

I didn't mind him going. I enjoyed being here at his house alone and there was something exciting about waiting for him to come home from work. Made me feel like a wife again. I cleaned the kitchen and dusted the downstairs while he was gone. And I had even prepared a broccoli and chicken casserole to put in the oven for dinner later. It felt domestically blissful.

His car rolled slowly to a stop and he got out. He was wearing a pastel yellow dress shirt with a light blue paisley tie and navy-blue pants. And his Ray-Ban sunglasses made him even more handsome. Every time I saw him, my heart fluttered like a school girl. He waved up at me and then reached into his backseat and pulled out his briefcase. He walked up on the porch and smiled.

"Is there more of that for me?" he said as he eyeballed my glass.

I laughed and jumped up to follow him inside to make him a glass too.

"So, how did the showing go?" I said as I poured the lemonade.

"They put in an offer, a good one." he smiled triumphantly.

I brought over a glass of lemonade and handed it to him as he loosened his tie. He leaned over and kissed me. Then sipped the lemonade.

"Mmmm, it's delicious, thank you," he smiled.

I reached up and helped him slip his necktie off. He set his glass on the counter. He looked at me and I could see the passion in his eyes. Then he pulled me in and kissed me again. His mouth tasted of sweetness and lemons.

He reached up and slipped the thin straps of my white linen tank top off of my shoulders. Then ran his tongue down my neck and I shivered with delight.

I unbuttoned his shirt and kissed the soft furls of hair on his chest. Then he undid the snap on my jean shorts. They fell to the floor and he lifted me up onto the countertop. He lifted my top over my head and unclasped my bra. Then ran his fingertips over my exposed breasts. Slipping off his pants, he entered me gently, looking into my eyes as we made love, never breaking his gaze from mine. The old countertop creaked underneath me. He was rhythmic and slow, easing in and out of me, his arm muscles flexed as I used them to hold onto. As the pace increased, I felt myself falling into that place of ecstasy and I cried out in pleasure.

Afterwards, he helped me down from the countertop. I went into the bathroom to freshen up and when I came out, he was not in the kitchen anymore. He always dressed so quickly after we made love whereas I would sometimes stay naked for a while. I guess he was a little shier than I was. He liked that I wasn't though, and let me know it with his satisfied smile.

I looked around for him inside and did not see him. He was sitting on the porch, and he was lost in thought. The screen door creaked as I opened it and came out. I sat down with him on the swing.

He put his arm around me.

"What do you think of us taking a little trip?" He said softly

We had never been on a trip together. In fact, I had not been on any trips since the trip to Cancun.

"What did you have in mind?" I was curious. Collin was always full of ideas and plans.

"I was thinking of Asheville, it's a bit of a drive but we could see the Fall leaves." he looked so sweet and innocent, like a little boy. My body still quivered from our activity in the kitchen, reminding me he was definitely not a boy.

"You know, that actually sounds wonderful," I sighed and snuggled up closer to him.

We went the very next weekend. It was the beginning of October and we had heard the leaves would be out in show. The Grand Asheville Resort is where we booked our stay. The hotel was five stars and it had an elegant lodge theme. When we arrived, there was a massive fireplace that was taller than me, that was bursting with warm flames. The smell of warm spice and vanilla was everywhere. Our room had a huge bed with a cranberry red and gold tapestry bedspread and large throw pillows with gold tasseled edges. In the room, there was some exotic sounding music playing from Bose speakers. The bottle of wine we had ordered in advance was there waiting. After we put our bags away, Collin opened the wine and poured us each a glass.

"To us!" He said as he clinked his glass to mine.

We spent several days in Asheville riding around and seeing the sights. The leaves were not a disappointment. I loved wearing sweaters and drinking warm apple cider. We went to a pumpkin patch and made our way through a corn maze. Each night we had dinner at the hotel restaurant. On our last night, we decided to try a local place called The Bier Yard. We had giant juicy hamburgers and tried several locally brewed beers.

Collin reached across the table and held my hand while we watched a football game one of their giant tv screens.

I saw out of the corner of my eye that he was staring at me. I turned to look at him.

"I want to take care of you, Sarah," his eyes had such sincerity in them.

"That's sweet, Collin, but I'm okay."

"...and I have you and Adam both helping me around the house," I don't know why I felt a little defensive suddenly.

"How do you take care of your expenses?" he peered intently at me.

"Thomas' life insurance money." I didn't like these questions

He looked perplexed.

"There's enough for you to live on, even after 14 years?"

"Yes, Thomas did up his policy quite a bit right before his death."

He paused for a moment.

"Don't you think that's odd that he upped the policy, right before he died?"

"No! Why would I think that was odd?" I felt my face burning.

"I would just think it was a strange coincidence that a man of his age would suddenly up his life insurance policy enough to provide for his wife for a lifetime right before he conveniently died."

I stood up and the chair made a loud screeching sound. Anger was pulsing through my body.

"Conveniently died?" I hissed.

"Oh my god, Sarah" "I didn't mean..."

I didn't hear what he said after that, I was already out the door.

I ran down the street and I was crying. I didn't know why. I was angry. Who did he think he was to question Thomas' motives? Why did he even bring it up? I had just gotten to the point where I didn't see Thomas every time I looked at Collin. And Now....oh I was just so angry.

It took Collin a few minutes to catch up to me. He had to pay our bill before leaving, giving me a head start. When he got to me, I was leaning against his locked car.

He approached me ruefully.

"Sarah, I am so sorry. I never meant to hurt you." He pushed my hair from my face and wiped the tears from my cheeks.

"I just want to take care of you, and to be honest; I am a little jealous that Thomas, even from the grave, is doing it better than I can. It isn't easy living in his shadow."

My emotions immediately shifted.

"I know, I overreacted too..." I looked down at the pavement. "You just have no idea what I have been through all these years without Thomas, and not to mention what the insurance agency put me through right after Thomas died. Questioning me and saying it was strange how 'he mysteriously died right after getting the policy increase.' It just triggered something in me when you said it too. And I'm sorry."

He reached out and pulled me close and then hugged me tightly.

I knew he felt terrible for what had happened between us. And I just couldn't stay mad at him any longer. But after we got back from the trip, I was a little more distant. I wasn't trying to punish him at all. I was just hearing the words that he said ring in my head over and over again. They were haunting me day and night. I had not really thought about it since Thomas died.

"I would just think it was a strange coincidence that a man of his age would suddenly up his life insurance policy to provide for his wife for a lifetime right before he conveniently died"

Now I couldn't get it off my mind. It was strange really. Now that I had time to think about it and wasn't so caught up in fresh blinding grief. Why did Thomas increase the policy and for so much? His original policy was for $500,000 and the new policy was 2.5 million dollars. I paid out all of his business expenses and paid off both of the houses. That took over half of it but still left me with a healthy balance. Enough for me to easily live on. It seems now that it was almost like he knew he was going to die. Like he had prepared for it in advance. Maybe he had a premonition? But if he did, he never mentioned it to me.

Thomas was an Investment Broker and ran his own firm. He specialized in small time clients. Helping the middle class prepare for retirement. He had a very strong relationship with almost all of his clients. Most of them attended his memorial service, in fact. He had a business partner, Neil Stetson. He and Neil started their own firm not long after college and they had a great relationship. They were best friends in fact. Neil was so devastated after Thomas' death, that he not only closed down the office but he also switched careers and started teaching business math at the community college. He sent an email occasionally to check in on the boys and me, but I hadn't spoken to him in person since we moved to Wilmington.

I didn't talk to anyone about the feelings of unrest that Collin had stirred up with his questions. I also did not bother mentioning my worries about this to Adam because he was too young at the time of Thomas' death to understand anything like that, and he would have no idea about what happened back then. So, he wouldn't be of any help to me trying to sort through my thoughts.

When I had lunch with Betsey, I mentioned it to her. She completely laughed it off. Thomas was that way, she had said. Always over prepared for everything. And she was right. Thomas

127

always did over prepare. Once, when we took the boys camping, he had packed three weeks' worth of food in his backpack, when we were only going on a weekend trip. When I asked him about it, he had said: "You have to expect the best but prepare for the worst and I always look out for my family!" He had smiled so big. He was proud of how well he took care of us.

After that lunch, I decided not to let it bother me anymore. I called Collin that night.

"Hi there stranger...," he said sheepishly.

"I miss you...." I said softly.

"I'll come over if you want me to..." I could tell he was hoping for a yes.

"Actually, I do want you to!" I responded enthusiastically.

Within 45 minutes, he was knocking on the door.

When I opened the door, he was standing there holding a movie rental and a bouquet of lilies.

I nearly leaped into his arms, causing him to drop the movie. In the porch light, we kissed and he hugged me tightly.

"I missed you, Sarah. More than you know."

After our trip, Collin sold three more houses. He was the featured agent at his agency now. There was even a blurb about him in the Wilmington Chronicle. They called him Wilmington's newest up and coming real estate professional. Once that ran in the paper, his client list grew dramatically. He was working nearly double the hours he was before. But he still made time for me. He always made me feel like a priority in his life.

I was testing the waters of what it was like to really start living again. I started going to the gym. I joined a little place down the road from me that hosted yoga three times a week. I loved riding the stationary bike there too. The effort I was putting in was starting to pay off. I had lost 5 pounds and was getting more toned.

I felt better too. I had stopped wondering so much about the Thomas and Collin connection. And I tried to be more present in the time I spent with Collin. Something I had learned in yoga. Being present in the moment was a big deal. And it helped me not dwell so much on the Thomas of the past and focus more on the Collin of today. Of course, I still had my slip-ups. I called out Thomas' name instead of Collin's when I was upstairs at my house and needed him to come and get something from the top of the closet for me. Thankfully he hadn't noticed. And I was still dreaming of Thomas, but not every night anymore. In some ways, I felt like he *was* slipping away. Yet there was in Collin, still something of Thomas that would never completely go away. Though the more time passed, the more I started to realize how different Collin and Thomas really were.

Adam and Emily were coming by to see me on a regular basis. I enjoyed their visits. We ate dinner together and played board games. Collin came when he had the time. We all had so much fun playing Monopoly and Scrabble. I was even talking to Blake on the phone once a week. The first time he called, I was shocked. But things were different between us now. Easier somehow. And we became very close. He told me all about Becca and his life out in California. He promised to bring her here to meet me during the holidays. And I couldn't wait. I was also excited for him to meet Collin. I'm sure he already knew I had a man friend, from Adam, but I had not told him anything about him myself, or about the eerie connections to Thomas. I didn't want to drive him away when we had just rekindled our relationship.

Emily and I became good friends. We both had a love for fine art and visited the Museum of Art in Raleigh several times together. It was only a short drive from Wilmington and we usually grabbed lunch while we were there. We laughed and talked together with the ease of lifelong friends. I hoped she was a keeper. I tried to talk to Adam about the idea of marrying her and he made it clear to me that it was not my business nor was it open for discussion. Emily would be graduating in the near future and I didn't want her to get away.

I was overstepping my bounds but my maternal instincts to protect Adam's happiness were strong. And they were perfect together. The dynamic between them had a flow that was more natural than most couples that had been together for years. She also brought out a side of Adam that I hadn't seen since before his father's death. I feared what would happen to him if they broke up.

My birthday was November 18th. I woke up early, and just as I poured a cup of coffee, the doorbell rang. I opened the door and no one was there. I looked down and there was a large closed basket on my porch. It was moving. And making sounds. It didn't take me long to figure out that there was something alive inside. I looked around confused and then I saw Collin standing in the driveway. And he was smiling.

I lifted the basket and sat it inside on the floor. I sat on the floor next to it, and Collin came in and sat down next to me.

"Well, aren't you going to open it?" he chided.

I slowly unlatched it and lifted the lid. And as soon as I did a ball of fur exploded out into my lap. The cutest little King Charles Cavalier puppy I had ever seen was licking my face all over. It was a little red colored male with white and black markings. I started to cry.

Collin immediately sat forward, "Oh honey, don't you like him?"

"I should've asked first." He looked scared.

"No, no," I choked.

"I love him! This is just the sweetest gift anyone has ever given me!"

My tears soon turned to laughter, as the puppy was licking me and rolling around in my lap with the biggest brown eyes I had ever seen.

We went out that morning and took him to Pets & More, and bought him a navy and white chevron collar and matching leash, a dog crate, food dishes, and some gourmet dog food. I was beside myself with joy. Even when he pee'd all over my lap in the car, I was still ecstatic.

"I love him, Collin...and I love you so much," I told him as we drove home.

He reached over and held my hand while the puppy christened it with kisses galore.

We named him Ash as a reminder of our trip to Asheville.

Pretty soon Thanksgiving had come and gone. And Christmas was right around the corner. Ash was becoming a pro at house training. It had been one week now with no accidents. I went through an entire bottle of Nature's Miracle since he arrived.

Collin was busy as ever, selling houses like hotcakes. It was strange to me how so many people bought houses around the holidays. Collin was doing so well that he was talking about starting his own real estate Brokerage office soon.

It was Friday night, a week before Christmas and we were going to the Holiday Flotilla, a Christmas Boat Parade. It was a Wilmington Christmas tradition. Adam and Emily were going with us. We found a spot that was not too crowded and watched the boats floating down the river all decked out in Christmas lights. Some white, some red and green. Some were even flashing. There were some boats with full Christmas trees on their deck. One big boat even had a palm tree decorated with flashing lights on it.

There were sailboats, yachts, fishing vessels, and small Jon boats. Each one had a different theme but all were fully lit up. We saw boats that were made into all sorts of things. There was a giant jellyfish, a train, a shark, a giant Santa Claus, an octopus, and a turtle. They were followed by a guy paddling a kayak with a Santa hat on. The crowd cheered for him the loudest. It was the first time I had seen this parade in all the years of living here. We laughed at some and applauded many of the floats. They had all put a lot of work into them and we certainly reaped the benefits of all their work.

When the last boat floated past, Collin and I said our goodbyes to Adam and Emily and headed back to my house. When we got back, we drank spiked eggnog and cuddled up by the fireplace. The fire was more for ambiance than heat. The nights were not cold enough yet to justify it. Ash played on the rug with the latest chew toy that Collin had brought for him. As much as Collin doted on Ash, I couldn't help but wonder if he had bought Ash for himself or for me. It made me laugh but I kept it inside. I definitely wouldn't call him out on it. I sat cuddled up to Collin. His strong chest made the perfect lounging spot. We sat quietly listening to Bing Crosby Christmas Songs. He was running his hands through my hair. I was letting it grow back out. He said he loved the way it was flowing down my back already. The moment was postcard perfect.

"Sarah, I need to ask you something." He turned me, so I was facing him. Then he reached into his pocket and pulled out a box. It was a tiny blue Tiffany's box wrapped in a white ribbon.

Collin shifted out from under me so that he could get on his knee.

My heart began pounding.

"Sarah, will you make me the happiest man in the whole world and marry me?" His eyes glistened with joy.

I sat staring back at him not saying a word. I was not sure what to say. My heartbeat was deafening and all I could see in front of me was Thomas. It was the day that he proposed to me. He had taken me out for a walk in the park, and then to dinner. For dessert, the waiter brought me a red velvet cupcake with a decadent whipped cream icing and on top of the cupcake was a beautiful 1-carat princess cut engagement ring. I never knew how he managed to buy that ring for me.

Thomas had come around the table, with everyone in the restaurant looking at him, gotten down on one knee and said to me, "Sarah, will you be my wife?"

I was so lost in my memories that I had forgotten about Collin. I looked at up and already knew that my hesitation had devastated him.

He stood up with tears in his eyes. He had a look I had never seen before. He dropped the ring box down on the floor.

"Collin.... I...." I could barely get his name out.

"You what?" he almost snarled. His eyes were ice cold.

I could not answer. I had no words.

"What is wrong with you Sarah!? Dammit! I can't help you fix your past and I definitely can't be who you want me to be. Why don't you wake up? I don't know how to help you. I have tried and nothing works. I don't know why I have not given up on you yet! All I know is that I can't get you out of my head. When I wake up every morning, I'm thinking of you. When I'm trying to work, I'm thinking of you. I can't sleep because I'm thinking of you. I need you, Sarah. And I love you more than you can imagine. But I need you to see me. *Me*, Sarah! See me for who I am right now. Here in front of you. You're so caught up in a memory and what you lost that it blinds you to what you have right now in front of you."

The thing was, he was right. Wasn't I just thinking of Thomas' proposal while he sat there holding a ring himself?

I started to cry.

"I'm sorry Collin, I don't know what's wrong with me."

"I am really mixed up; I just feel like something is strange. It feels like you somehow have Thomas inside of you...."

He instantly stepped back away from me. Wide-eyed and clearly disturbed.

"Thomas inside of me?" he stuttered.

"Sarah, I have tried to love you and I have hoped beyond hope that you could love me for me." He walked up and took me by the arms.

"I can never be Thomas; can you understand that?" his voice was loud and agitated.

"Why can't you just accept that? Why do you keep pushing for something that can't be there?" his eyes were etched in hurt.

"Collin, I do love you." I sobbed

"But only because I remind you of him, right?" he asked with a tone of mockery.

"No, that's not it!" I managed between sobs.

He came to me and held me then.

"Don't cry, Sarah. I'm really sorry I raised my voice. I guess I'm feeling desperate." He stroked my hair gently, holding me tight to his chest. I could hear his heartbeat, steady and strong.

"I'm sorry that I'm so messed up." I was still crying.

But I honestly meant it. What *was* wrong with me? Why couldn't I let Thomas go? And why do I keep putting him between us?

He picked up the ring box off of the floor, held it for a moment and then handed the box to me. I clutched it in my hands while tears were streaming down my face.

"Why don't you hold onto to it for a bit?" he said softly.

"There's no rush." He looked at me with such love and tenderness.

"And when you are ready, I'll be here."

He kissed my forehead and then stepped back.

"I think I am going to go home now and give you some time to digest all of this." His eyes were soft again.

"I'll call you tomorrow," he said as he walked toward the door with Ash on his heels.

"I do love you, Sarah, more than you can ever know."
He closed the door quietly.

Ash was scratching and whining at the door wanting him to come back inside. I did too. I hated myself right now. Nothing felt right anymore.

I sank to the floor and stared at the little blue box in my hands.

Chapter 20

———— ✦ ————

I waited with Emily at ILM airport for Blake's plane to touch down. It was the day before Christmas Eve. I was really excited. I hadn't seen my brother in over two years.

I kept walking impatiently over to the tv monitors with the flight information waiting for an update on the landing.

"Quit pacing!" Emily rolled her eyes at me. She had been complaining quite a bit lately. And everything I did seemed to get on her nerves.

Soon the monitor said that Blake's plane had landed and we quickly made our way over to Gate B.

People began pouring out of the corridor. I started scanning faces for Blake. Families were hugging and businessmen were walking briskly past. Finally, I saw him. And he had a gorgeous brunette on his arm. That must be Becca. Man, he wasn't joking about how beautiful she was.

Blake came in and gave me a big bro hug.

"What's up brother?!" Blake looked good. He had filled out and put on some muscle since moving to California. What happened to my scrawny baby brother?

"Glad to see you! This is Becca!" Blake turned toward her and beamed.

She had long curly dark hair. Tan and super long legs. Green eyes and the softest looking pink lips that I had ever seen. I felt myself staring a little too long and had to break my gaze. I mumbled a greeting and then suddenly I remembered Emily.

"Ummm, yeah, this is Emily." I could feel my face burning with embarrassment. I couldn't turn to look at Emily's face. I already knew she was pissed.

Blake came in and gave Emily a big hug and then Becca did the same.

Friendly girl. Wish she would've given me a hug.

We walked over to the baggage claim. The conveyer belt groaned as it started to move. We stood together making small talk while watching large duffels, black Samsonite suitcases, and even a pink cheetah print bag roll by. Finally, Blake reached out and grabbed a backpack and a large turquoise suitcase off the line. He turned and looked at me.

"Man, it is good to see you brother!"

"Yeah, me too." I smiled.

"So, you guys hungry?" It was 9 pm here, and their stomachs were on Pacific time.

We agreed on North's Bar and Grille. It was a place that was mostly frequented by locals. A laid back traditional bar and grill atmosphere.

The place sat one street off from the ocean, and when we got out of the car, we could smell the salt in the air. We walked in and the old wood floors creaked as we crossed to get to our table.

We grabbed a table in the back and a tall, middle-aged brunette with a deep southern drawl took our order. She called us darlin' and smiled with tobacco stained teeth. Blake and Becca wanted fish and chips for dinner. This place hailed local catch. We all four ordered beers on tap. I always ordered the local craft brews. They were better than the mainstream beers. We sat and talked about the weather and southern hospitality while they ate.

Becca was quiet. I wasn't sure if she was shy around new people, or just not a talkative person. There was a vast difference between her and Emily, who was at the moment dominating the conversation asking Blake questions about school and living out on the West Coast. She didn't say much of anything to Becca who was listening intently. I was struggling because I kept catching myself staring at Becca. She was wearing a white low-cut tank top and a jean mini skirt. She had bracelets on both wrists and white painted nails. And she had a silver surfboard charm around her neck and a small sunshine tattoo on her chest right above her breast. I had to make a concerted effort not to look. Finally, I turned my chair, so it was directly facing Blake. I didn't know why I was so mesmerized by Becca. She was undeniably gorgeous, but I was in love with Emily. Maybe it was because Emily's attitude lately was wearing thin. Or because we hadn't had sex in 3 weeks. Either way, I needed to knock this crap off.

Blake leaned back in his chair and put his hands behind his head. He told us about school, how his professors said he had a natural knack for business, and how he was already talking to several Fortune 500 companies about his career path after school. I was proud of my baby brother. He was all grown up now.

I had wondered if Blake would ever get his act together and it seems that he had. And he certainly had good taste in women. I hoped Blake hadn't noticed my admiration of Becca.

Becca whispered something in Blake's ear and then got up and went to the jukebox. She was leaning over the jukebox and dancing. Then she put on some Bob Marley.

Blake looked over at her and smiled.

"Man, I really love her Adam."

"Hey, that's great!" I patted him on the arm.

"She seems like a sweet girl!" I was genuinely happy for him.

But then Becca came back and sat on his lap and I cringed with jealousy.

"Sooo, how's Mom?" he looked overly concerned

"Well, she's doing great actually." I nodded as if to reassure him.

"In fact, she has a boyfriend." I had to laugh a little. Our mom having a boyfriend was something I was still getting used to.

Blake looked completely stunned. He looked as if someone just told him aliens had landed in the parking lot.

"What?" he stuttered.

"What do you mean a boyfriend?" His face was white.

I laughed a little. "You'll see soon enough!"

I was actually enjoying torturing him. Just like when we were kids and I told him that there were bears outside that would eat him up. He had nightmares for a month after that. Mom was so mad, but Dad said it was just boys being boys, so I didn't get punished.

Blake looked less than thrilled. I decided not to tell him about how mom thought that the new guy was actually Dad reincarnated, or some crazy idea like that. He was having enough trouble digesting the boyfriend part.

I looked at my watch. It was nearly midnight. I had texted Mom earlier and told her we were going out. She wasn't going to wait up for us.

"You guys want to crash at my place?" I asked the question directly of Blake. Trying to keep the thought of Becca coming home to my place, out of my mind.

"Then we can head over to Mom's in the morning," I added.

They agreed, so we paid our tab to the waitress, who kept giving Blake flirtatious smiles.

And then we headed back to the apartment.

Thank god Emily had taken that cat home. The last thing I wanted was for Blake and Becca to smell cat crap the second they got in there.

"Cool place, brother!" Blake walked around the apartment looking at everything.

I pulled the sofa bed out, and Emily got them blankets and pillows. She hadn't said a word on the drive home.

She walked into the kitchen to get a glass of water. I followed in behind her.

"You staying tonight too?" I asked half hoping she would say no.

She glared at me.

"Why? don't you want me to?" sarcasm was apparently another gift of hers.

She knew, that I knew, that she was mad. But I'd still deny it, and she knew that too. I mean, why was she angry anyway? I'm just a guy; it's not like I slept with Becca or something. I was just looking. Good thing she can't read minds.

"Of course, I do baby!" I tried to put my arms around her and she slipped out from underneath them.

"Well, actually, I am going home!" her face was tight. I was glad she was leaving because I didn't want to hear her bitch at me when we got in my room. And I knew it was coming. I could feel her anger seething out at me the whole night

She grabbed her purse, and went over and wished Blake and Becca goodnight. She left without looking back at me. And I didn't even bother to walk her out, which I usually did. I felt sick to my stomach. What was going so wrong with us?

I showed Blake and Becca how to use the TV set and headed to bed. I had to push away the thought of what it might be like to lie next to Becca in bed.

I crawled into my bed around 1 am. I laid there tossing and turning until 4 am. I couldn't fall asleep. I kept thinking about Emily and me. We had a huge fight a few weeks ago about marriage. Emily was graduating in the Spring and was already talking to Architectural firms all over the nation. The one she was mainly interested in was in Boulder, Colorado. She had interviewed with them the week before. She felt like she would probably receive an official offer from them in January sometime since they had already mentioned a position to her.

We were sitting on my couch watching Dexter reruns and she looked over at me.

"Do you love me, Adam?"

"Of course, I do, babe, what kind of question is that?" I half laughed.

"We really need to talk about our future together. Every time I bring it up, you change the subject. I need to know where we stand." She looked adamant.

"Do you want to get married?" Her words hung in the air like a storm cloud getting ready to ascend.

I panicked immediately. My heart was racing. Marriage? I wasn't the marrying kind. I mean, I hadn't even thought of dating anyone seriously before Emily and now she wants to get married!

I tried to steady my voice.

"I don't know Emily. I don't think I'm ready for marriage, I mean I have to finish out my Master's degree and then work on my Ph.D." I was trying to sound legitimate.

"You could go to school in Colorado..." she looked at me hopefully.

"No way! I'm not leaving my mom and going halfway across the country!" My voice rose a level or two. Who did she think she was to ask that of me?

"I would be willing to give up the Boulder job, and find a position close by if I knew we were serious about each other....." Her face was soft and open.

Dammit, why was she making this so hard? Why couldn't she just scream and yell about marrying her like a typical girl? That would make saying no so much easier.

"Babe, I am just not the marrying kind of guy." Yep, I said it, and it was too late to take it back.

It was out there suspended between us now.

"Not the marrying kind!?" her voice nearly screeched in disbelief.

Here comes the crazy girl behavior. I braced myself for it.

But instead, she stood up with tears rolling down her face.

"What you mean to say, is *I* am not the kind of girl you would marry!"

"Now come on Emily!" I stood up too. "I love you, isn't that enough?"

I wasn't sure what else to say. I couldn't say what she wanted to hear.

She looked at me standing there in my silence, with a look of horror on her face.

She ran out of the door and straight to her car. I followed right behind her, but she started the car engine and backed it up, nearly running me over. She drove off and I stood there in the parking lot in my boxers feeling like a real shit.

142

After that, things were not the same. She didn't mention it again, but the dynamic between us was stale at best.

I laid there in the bed for hours thinking of the good times we had together. All the great sex we had. She was a great girl. A fun girl. Well at least, she *was*. I don't know why I didn't want to marry her. But she had no right to demand it from me either.

She just didn't understand me at all. I never even wanted a serious relationship. I saw what losing Dad did to Mom, and I never wanted another person to have that much control over my life. I wasn't about to lose my identity to anyone. She would have to take me as I am, or not at all. But despite all my macho self-talk, deep down inside, I knew the truth. I would be lost without her. I wasn't going to admit it though. Ever.

Luckily my west coast guests slept in, so I was able to stay in bed until 10 am. I checked my phone and was surprised to find that were no messages from Emily. She usually would have texted me by now.

I texted mom and told her we would be over in a bit. She said she and Collin were just making a Christmas Eve Brunch for all of us. I went to wake Blake and Becca up. I jumped on top of Blake and gave him a noogie, just like I did when we were kids. He punched me square in the stomach. We both were laughing. Becca rolled over and looked at me. Damn, she even looked good in the morning.

We drove over to mom's house. And of course, Collin's car was there. And Blake asked about the car as soon as he saw it.

"It's mom's *boyfriend*'s car," I snickered.

Blake shuddered. As soon as we pulled up, Mom came running out the front door and into the driveway.

She hugged Blake for a long time, and when she finally let go, he introduced her to Becca.

Mom was very likable, so I knew that she and Becca would get along just fine. In fact, she and Emily hung out regularly. Even before Emily had brought up marriage, mom was pressuring me to pop the question. I couldn't help but wonder if mom had any influence on Emily pressuring me.

Mom immediately hugged Becca too. Becca was smiling. Man, she was so beautiful.

We went inside and the delicious smell of food met us at the door along with mom's new dog Ash.

Becca bent down and kissed the puppy. "What a cute little guy!"

Collin came out from the kitchen wearing an apron. Very domestic looking.

Mom introduced him to Blake and Becca. I watched Collin and he seemed to be unaffected by Becca's beauty. I couldn't help but half wonder if he were gay. Who could be unaffected by Becca?

Mom took Becca up to Blake's room so she could see where they would be staying. Blake and I followed Collin into the kitchen to pitch in. Collin gave Blake a basket of croissants and a carafe of orange juice. He handed me a giant, piping hot, bowl of shrimp and grits.

He followed behind us with a bottle of champagne and a sizable bowl of fruit. We were eating outside. The temperature was in the high 60's and with the sun, the weather was ideal. The table was set for 6.

Mom and Becca came out right behind us with Ash under their feet.

"Where's Emily?" Mom looked at me concerned.

"Let me go call her." I realized I still hadn't heard from her and it was nearly 11 am.

I stepped inside and dialed Emily's number.

"Hello," she said unenthusiastically.

"Hey, I haven't heard from you today. Are you okay?"

"I'm fine," she responded bluntly.

"We're having brunch at my mom's and she was wondering where you were."

"At least someone cares about whether I'm there or not," she huffed.

"So, are you coming?" I didn't like the game she was playing. I was met with silence.

"Emily?"

"I'm not coming Adam," she said defiantly.

"Why not!?" I was getting irritated.

"We can talk later, I gotta go." and she hung up on me.

Well damn.

I went back outside, and everyone was drinking mimosas and laughing.

Mom looked at me. "Is she coming?"

"No, she has a family thing to do this morning." I didn't know why I was covering for her.

We ate the shrimp and grits after explaining them to Becca. She had never even heard of grits before. Collin had gone down to the docks this morning and purchased the shrimp from a local fisherman. Then he had prepared the dish himself. The croissants were warm, slathered in butter, and melted in your mouth. All the fruit was fresh cut. Everything was delicious, to say the least.

Collin and Becca had a lot to talk about, both being from California. Blake joined in the conversation quite a bit. He included himself as a resident there, even though he had only lived there two years.

Mom sat watching all of us. She had a look of such love on her face. I knew she was happy that Blake was home. Ash was under the table begging for handouts. I saw Collin slip him a bite of croissant.

Blake and Collin hit it off big time. I actually felt a little jealous of how well they got along. They laughed and talked together all day like they had known each other their whole lives. Becca and Mom got along pretty well too. Becca was more open and talkative to Mom. She told mom about her childhood and how her family always took a picnic lunch to the beach on Christmas Eve. This was her first Christmas away from her family. She was really missing them. Later in the day, she Facetimed them on her phone. We were all introduced. She was the oldest of 4 kids, all girls. The youngest was 4. All the girls were just as beautiful as Becca. Her mom was beautiful too. Good genes. And they seemed like a very close-knit family. Something I didn't really understand. It was a different dynamic for us growing up with Mom so sad all the time. Then I wondered about Emily and what she was doing. I didn't like being away from her like this. Why was she trying to punish me? I felt like a 5th wheel in this group. Mom came up and hugged me tightly.

"Is everything okay, honey?" she sensed something wasn't right.

"I screwed up big time with Emily." I looked down with shame.

"What happened?" Mom's face had a look of tenderness and understanding.

"I told her I didn't want to marry her...," I answered shamefully.

"So, why *don't* you want to marry her, Adam?" That zinged me.

I don't know how she did it, but Mom always had a way of asking just the right question that would bring you straight to the heart of the issue.

"I don't know, Mom." I shrugged.

"Well, maybe that's something you need to be asking yourself. And when you figure that out, you will know what you need to do. That will make you feel a lot better about everything."

She was right. I needed to spend some time figuring out exactly what I wanted out of life. I always thought I knew. But apparently, I had no idea.

The rest of the day passed with ease. That evening, we gathered around the Christmas tree and Collin built a fire for us. Mom put on a Time Life's Christmas album and we opened gifts. Mom gave Blake and me gift cards to Bob's Sports Store, plus each of us a bottle of the new Chanel cologne. She gave Becca a tan leather-bound journal with a flower embossed on it and a silver pen set. Becca seemed to love it.

Mom went under the tree and got a small box for Collin. I suddenly realized that I hadn't seen them cuddling or kissing all day. That was the status quo for those two so it was definitely odd that they weren't. Maybe I wasn't the only one having relationship problems. I watched their faces for any signs of trouble.

She walked over and handed him the box. He reached up and pulled her down onto his lap. She laughed. I was relieved to see that interaction; I didn't think mom could handle a breakup. He opened his gift. It was a hand carved wooden sailboat. He smiled at her and then told her that she would have to wait for her gift until tomorrow morning.

Blake and Becca exchanged gifts by the fireplace with Ash jumping all around them. They were sitting close and giggling. I didn't even wait to see what the gifts were. I walked into the kitchen to call Emily again. She didn't answer. My heart sunk in my chest. What the heck?

I decided to stay the night at mom's and slept in my childhood bed. I laid there alone and wondered what Emily's point was right now. This just wasn't like her. Well maybe, it was like the *new* her.

I could hear whispering and laughing coming from the other bedrooms. I wondered if Blake and Becca were having sex, and I couldn't help but wonder what Becca looked like naked.

I fell asleep shortly after midnight. I didn't hear Santa or reindeer feet on the roof but I did hear my phone ding at 3 am. It was a text from Emily. Simply stated.

"We need to talk."

I tried to call and she didn't answer.

I texted her and she said she would come by here sometime tomorrow. I couldn't go back to sleep after that.

Christmas mornings did not hold that childhood magic anymore but it was nice to wake up to the smell of pancakes and bacon. I was exhausted. 2 nights in a row with only a few hours of sleep.

We all ate breakfast together and Blake and I talked about squeezing in a trip to Crowder's Mountain to go rock climbing before he leaves. I was trying not to think about Emily. I knew whatever she had to say, wasn't going to be good.

"Rock climbing?" mom looked horrified.

"I don't want you to go rock climbing!" She looked over at Collin for support, but he looked just as baffled as we did.

"Why not?" I asked defiantly.

"You could be injured or killed...." She trailed off.

"I just don't want you to go," she looked dead serious. Blake reached over and touched her hand gently.

"Mom, we will be fine."

"We will be extra careful, but if it bothers you too much, we just won't go."

Since when is Blake the thoughtful son?

"Blake, I really want to go, man!" I interrupted.

"Do neither of you remember your father's injury?" She looked back and forth between us.

"He was lead climbing and one of his fixed pitons failed and he fell down the cliff gouging open his left butt cheek right through his jeans. He had a massive 4-inch scar from it with giant incision marks all the way down the side of it from where they had to sew him up. It looked like a giant centipede. I used to joke and call him centipede butt. We laughed about that, but in all seriousness, he could've been killed. If that rock had punctured his lung instead of his behind.... He never rock climbed again after that. I am just so terrified of what could happen to you boys."

I kind of remembered the scar from when I was super little but honestly, I would've never remembered it, if she hadn't brought it up. Blake said he didn't remember it at all.

Collin spoke up.

"Sarah, I think you should let the boys go if they want to." Mom immediately cut her eyes at him.

"Rock climbing accidents happen, yes, but they're not that common, especially if you are vigilant about safety. I think these guys would be extra cautious especially after the story about their dad. And plus, that would give you some time to spend with Becca and get to know her better."

Mom's faced softened and she smiled at Collin. He knew exactly what to say to calm her down.

"I guess you're right," she smiled at us too, but she still looked worried.

We spent the day watching old Christmas movies and when it got dark, we drove around and looked at Christmas lights. We got back around 9 pm. I still had not heard from Emily.

I called her phone, and she answered on the first ring.

"I was actually just going to call you, and see if this was a good time to come by?" her voice sounded strained.

"Sure, come on over," I sounded calm but inside I was panicking.

"Okay wait for me outside," she hung up without a goodbye again.

I sat on mom's front porch waiting for Emily to come. I shivered. I didn't know if it was nervousness or the cold.

Her little white Toyota Camry pulled in and she motioned for me to come to the car.

I got in the passenger's seat.

"I'm sorry I didn't come until now. I just needed time to think about how to say this to you." she started. Her face looked sad.

"Look Em; I am sorry about everything..." I tried to say, but she interrupted me.

"Don't Adam. Just don't complicate this any more than it already it is."

What the heck did that mean? I just looked at her.

"I think we should break up," Did she just say break up?

"What do you mean break up?" my voice had a sharp edge to it.

"I can't do this anymore. I'm taking that job in Boulder if they make the offer," she was looking down at her lap.

"I don't want you to go." I felt my chest tightening.

"It is for the best, Adam..." Her eyes were the saddest I have ever seen.

"I do love you, Adam, but I can't be with you. You have never given yourself completely to me. You are always holding back. It makes me feel like I am just there with you out of convenience. You are always so preoccupied with what's going on with you. You just don't see me. And the whole marriage thing was just a real eye-opener for me. I by no means wanted to force you into marriage, but it was a wake-up call. We are just so different and we want different things out of life, clearly. Rather than keep building up resentment toward you and see the relationship through to its inevitable end, I thought it was better to go ahead and end it here. I don't like the person I have been the last few weeks. I've been bitter and angry. We will both just be happier if we go our separate ways." Her face was stone cold.

I sat listening to her and felt like I was talking to a stranger. I had no idea that she had felt that way. I was crazy about her. How could she not know that?

"Oh, come on Em, you don't mean that!" I leaned in to kiss her and she jerked back.

"Adam! I'm serious! It's over!" Tears started streaming down her face.

"Dammit Emily, this is fucked up!"

"Get out Adam!"

I sat there and didn't make a move to get out.

"ADAM! GET OUT!" I almost jumped out of my skin. Why the fuck did she have to yell?

I opened the door and got out. I barely got the door closed before she was backing out of the driveway and then she was gone. I watched her lights disappear into the night.

What the hell did she mean that she was just there for convenience? What the hell is convenient about a girlfriend? I mean, they're always fucking wanting something. They're never satisfied. Even the best girlfriend is a pain in the ass. Then now she breaks up with me because I won't marry her? I mean, she has been nothing but a bitch the last month and she wants to know why I am not giving her more attention? Well, screw her! I don't need this shit!

I went and got into my car and screeched out of the driveway. I didn't even tell anyone I was leaving. I just needed to drive. What a fucking Christmas this had been!

I sped down Pine Grove Road. I was going 70 mph in a 45 mph zone and I didn't care. I was trying to escape what I was feeling on the inside. How could I live without Emily? I didn't think she'd ever break up with me. And yet she did. I never loved anyone the way I loved Emily. How could she leave me and move to Colorado? My stomach was in knots. My thoughts were racing. I was angry and I was sad. The two emotions were indiscernible at the moment.

I rounded the curves too fast and almost went off the side. I wasn't paying attention at all and with the speed of my car, I didn't see the truck pull out of me. Suddenly I heard a smashing sound and my car was spinning and then flipping end over end. Everything seemed to move in slow motion.

Then the blackness came.

Chapter 21

Everyone had gone to bed. It had been a wonderful Christmas. Collin was asleep in my bed upstairs. He had been so sweet to me, considering my hurting him over his proposal. He hadn't brought it up once since that night. He just went on like nothing had happened. I wish I could do the same.

I sat with Ash in my lap, staring at the Christmas tree. I couldn't fall asleep. So, I came downstairs to sit and think. All the lights were off except the tree. This was the last night the lights would be on for this season and I wanted to enjoy it. It was always a little depressing to take down the holiday lights and decorations.

This morning Collin had given me a box of flower seeds he had ordered directly from Holland for me to put in my garden in the Spring. I loved the gift so much and he knew I would.

Collin and Blake really hit it off. I was very pleased. In fact, He and Blake had gotten along so well; I could not help but let it refuel the belief in my theories about Thomas. Thomas and Blake were always so close. Blake would naturally bond with Collin. Of course, that complicated my emotions about the engagement ring. I wished I just had an answer. Was he Thomas? It seemed impossible but completely possible at the same time. I had even explored the possibility that Collin was actually Thomas somehow, and suffering from amnesia, but he claimed to remember his entire life, although he didn't speak much about his childhood or his younger years. He said that he chose to put those days behind him and the person he was then didn't exist anymore. He was adamant that he suffered no memory losses. I wondered if he could see the ruse behind all my questions or did he think I was just a pushy woman. I have been living in this charade of normalcy with him for months now.

Playing a game that only I knew the rules to. But who was I fooling really? Me or Collin? Was he even fooled at all? He loved me so much. Unconditionally. I wish I could give him that same level of love too and just open myself to Collin fully. But to do so, I would have to let go of Thomas entirely, and I just couldn't do it. Then I instantly thought of the dream where Thomas had told me on the mountaintop, to let him go and I shuddered. Maybe I just needed some time on my own for a while. Maybe that would help me think clearer.

I went into the kitchen and made myself a cup of tea; I often drank chamomile tea when my mind raced like this at night.

I was a little concerned about Adam too. He left earlier without saying goodbye. I think Emily came by too. I assumed they left together. But I had an uneasy feeling for sure.

I sat on a bar stool at the kitchen counter and sipped my tea. Ash was laying at my feet. I looked up and Collin was standing in the doorway.

"You can't sleep?" he smiled sleepily.

"No, not really, do you want some tea?" I offered.

He was about to answer me but turned suddenly because he heard the front screen door creak. Then there was a loud knock.

He went to the door and I followed quickly behind him. When he opened the door, two uniformed police officers were standing there.

Ash started barking. Collin picked him up and held him.

My heart was in my throat.

"Are you the parents of Adam Avery?"

I stepped forward. My heart was in my throat.

"He's my son. Is he okay?" My voice was shaking

"He has been in a car accident and has been taken to New Hanover Regional Hospital."

"Oh my god, is he okay?" I shrieked.

"I'm sorry ma'am but we don't have any information on his condition." I could not read the expressions on the officer's faces. They probably had to do this all the time.

I ran back inside without saying another word. I went up to Blake's room and banged on the door.

"Blake!" "Blake!" I yelled.

"Yeah, mom?" I heard him say groggily from the other side.

"Your brother has been in an accident!"

I heard thudding and he opened the door.

"Oh my god, is he okay!?" Blake's hair was sticking straight up. He always got the worst bed head.

"They didn't tell me, I am leaving now to go to the hospital."

"I'm coming with you!" He threw on a t-shirt and gym shorts.

I grabbed my keys and started toward the door. Collin stopped me.

"Give me two minutes, and I'll drive you guys there."

"No! I need to go now!" my voice was so high pitched, I didn't even recognize it.

"You are *not* driving in this state of mind!" he said it so firmly, that I didn't even question it.

Becca came down the stairs with her hair in a bun, wearing a t-shirt and sweats. Eyeliner was smeared under eyes.

We went outside and got into Collin's car. He came out right after us.

We drove fast through the dark empty streets and got to the hospital pretty quickly. We parked and went straight inside to the main desk. They told us that Adam was in the ICU.

Thank god, he was alive at least.

We went up to the 5th floor and walked over to the nurse's station. They led us into the family waiting room for the ICU. The nurse was a beautiful black woman with a sweet, comforting voice. She told us to wait and the doctor would come and talk to us.

None of us spoke a word while we were waiting. I felt like my life was suspended entirely in mid-motion.

After about 30 minutes, an extremely young-looking doctor came into the room, he didn't even look old enough to be out of high school much less a practicing physician. He had jet black hair and a strong jawline.

"Hello, are you the family of Adam Avery?" His voice even sounded young.

We all gathered around this young boy whose next words would either restore or destroy my world.

"My name is Dr. Matt Andrews, and I have been overseeing the treatment of your son. I have to tell you that Adam is in critical condition and is in a persistent coma. He has suffered a Traumatic Brain Injury. He also has a punctured lung and spleen. Both of his arms are broken as well as his nose."

He said it all so matter of factly.

I was overwhelmed by the gravity of all he had just said. Collin put his arm around me.

"Is he going to be okay?" My voice still had that high pitch tone.

"I can't say, I have seen patients worse than this comeback, and patients much better off not make it. I am sorry I really wish I could tell you more."

I couldn't help but wonder if he was even old enough to be credible.

"When can we see him?" I was holding back a waterfall of tears.

"It's past visiting hours, but under these circumstances, we can allow you to go in 2 at a time for 5 minutes only."

He looked at us with gentle, understanding brown eyes. I stepped forward, and Collin and Blake did too. I looked at him and then looked at Blake. Collin immediately stepped back.

"Of course, his brother should go in..." Collin looked morose.

Blake and I walked into a curtain-walled room. Adam was lying there silent while machines kept him alive. Pumping and clicking. He had tubes and wires all over him. As soon as I saw him, I gasped and choked back a scream. His face was black and blue. Both of his arms were in casts. I walked over to the bed and leaned over my son. My tears finally broke through and fell onto his white sheets.

"I'm here Adam. I love you so much! Please pull through this; I need you to come back to me!"

I stepped back so Blake could get to his brother. Blake leaned over and said something I couldn't hear. Then we stood there together, arm in arm until the nurse came in and said: "I am sorry, but you need to go now."

We went back to the waiting room. I sat down on a small couch with Collin.

"How did he look?" His face looked worn with worry.

I just shook my head and started crying again.

Blake didn't say a word. He just sat down in a chair and put his face in his hands. Becca pulled up a chair next to him and rubbed her hand on his back.

Suddenly, I thought about Emily. Oh my god Emily! I wondered if she was with him in the accident?! I looked at my phone; it was 2 am. I dialed her number with my heart in my throat. When she picked up, it sounded like she was sleeping.

"Emily, its Sarah. Adam has been in an accident." I was crying when I said it.

"Oh my god, is he okay?" her voice was cracking.

"He is in a coma. They don't know what's going to happen." I said almost in a whisper.

"I'm coming!" she said. I could tell she was crying.

The days passed slowly. I stayed in the room with Adam whenever they'd allow it. Emily came and took shifts too. We sat and talked to him. Emily even sang to him. We brushed his hair.

People sent cards and flowers, but they were kept outside of his room to prevent any contamination. His face was beginning to heal, but he looked so different since they shaved his beard. He looked like a little boy again.

He began to stabilize, but he didn't wake up. They moved him to the 4th floor and put us in a regular hospital room. All his life-giving machines came with him. We brought all of his flowers and cards in there. Emily and I settled into our new routine. I stayed days, and she stayed nights. She had school during the day, and I didn't sleep well on the hospital pull out.

Blake and Becca had gone back to California. They had extended their trip by a week in the hopes of Adam waking up. I promised to call as soon as he did. The doctors made no promises of that though.

Collin came by regularly to see Adam and me. He was working extremely long days, so I hadn't seen much of him since the accident. He had opened his own office and was super busy, and I was too tired at night to do anything except eat and go to bed. This was not what I was thinking of when I said I needed time on my own to think. But Adam wasn't much of a conversationalist these days, so I had lots of time to think. But thinking was exactly what I was avoiding. I didn't need any erratic thoughts on my mind right now. I needed to focus on Adam and giving him all the positive energy that I could. So, I opted for crossword puzzles and Anita Shreve novels to fill the quiet days. I hired a pet sitter to come to the house and stay with Ash during the day. He was always happy to see me when I got home. And his puppy kisses were a warm welcome.

Emily was looking pretty worn too. She always seemed like she had something on her mind that she wanted to talk to me about but then she would look at Adam and tear up. Never saying what was on her mind. Even if I asked, she would deny needing to talk. So, I let it be. This was hard enough on her. I didn't want to intrude. One day she came in earlier than usual. She had brought both of us Lattes from North Coffee House on Front street.

"Sarah, can I ask you a question?" she started with hesitation.

"Of course, you can." I smiled gently.

"Is it possible to be happy, loving a man who cannot give you all of himself?"

I paused because I knew this question was about my son who lay here helpless, not even able to take his own breaths.

"Well, I think that depends on you. If you are willing to accept what he is able to give and you can let go of any expectations of anything else, then my answer is, yes. I am not saying that a situation like that always ends well, but I'm saying yes, you can be happy loving him."

"Okay......" she trailed off.

I waited to see if she wanted to say more and she didn't.

"Emily, Adam is a complicated man. There is a lot more going on under the surface than you realize. And I know that he loves you very much. He has never truly loved a woman until he met you. No matter what is coming out of his mouth, his heart tells the truth."

I could see that something clicked in Emily at that moment and she smiled.

"Thank you, Sarah." She came up and hugged me tightly. I saw that she had tears in her eyes.

The next day made exactly six weeks since the accident. Adam showed no signs of life, aside from the clicking and popping of his life support machines. The doctors had removed his casts early this morning. His body had healed up completely. Now, if only he would wake up.

I stood looking out the window. It was nearly mid-February. And Valentine's day was just around the corner. The hospital had red paper hearts decorated down all the hallway walls. Collin hadn't mentioned Valentine's day at all, but I figured he was thinking about it and that ring in the blue box that neither of us had mentioned since the night he gave it to me. I felt strange about how to face Valentine's day myself because Thomas and I celebrated Valentine's Day in the Bulgarian tradition. Thomas' grandmother was Bulgarian. And in Bulgaria, Valentine's Day is known as Winemaker's Day. Their way of celebrating Valentine's Day was for lovers to toast each other with a glass of local wine. We did it every single year. We would go and buy a bottle of local wine, and with our toasts, we would tell each other what we appreciated about the other. And even after he died, I kept it up. I would talk to his picture and tell him how much I missed him. It was now a sad holiday for me. And I didn't know how to fit Collin into it or how to include him in that tradition without feeling like I was betraying Thomas. The whole thing just felt strange.

I walked over to Adam's bed and fussed with his sheets. Out of the corner of my eye, I thought I saw movement. I looked again, and his toes were moving under the blankets, and I pushed the call button for the nurse, and I saw his eyelids flutter.

The nurses came right in, and soon a whole team of people gathered around him. They asked me to step back. My heart was racing with excitement. I texted Emily, Collin, and Blake. He's awake!

I tried to peer through the wall of people to see my son but I couldn't. Eventually, they started walking away, and the doctor came in. I was able to make my way back to Adam's side. His eyes were wide open, and he kept coughing. The doctor said that was because of the tracheal tube and it was nothing to worry about. Adam's blue eyes met mine, and I started to cry. He whispered, and I bent over to hear him.

"Where's Emily?" his voice was a whisper.

"She will be here soon!" I patted his arm.

He smiled then winced with pain.

The doctor was still looking him over.

"I love you, Mom." his voice was hoarse.

"I love you too, honey." I squeezed his hand, and he squeezed back. I was overcome with joy.

The doctor was asking him questions to check his mental clarity. He seemed to be perfectly fine.

161

Then the doctor announced: "He seems to be doing fantastic. I can't find a single thing wrong!" he smiled at me.

He knew those were the words I had been waiting to hear.

"Everything has healed up nicely, and now that he is awake, I think he will be able to go home in a day or two." He looked happy himself at the news.

Just then, Emily walked, well ran, in through the door. She rushed to Adam's side. She was crying and kissing his face. He was crying too. I walked out of the room and headed home. I felt like they needed some time to themselves. I ran into Collin in the hospital atrium. Someone was playing a soft melody on the Grand Piano. I had almost missed him. He was on his way up to see Adam. I updated him on what the doctor said, and he looked so relieved.

"He is with Emily right now, and I think they need some time alone. And...I was actually headed home myself."

"Want some company?" he offered hopefully.

"No thanks, I need some alone time myself." I saw him grimace.

I felt bad for turning him away, but I needed time to think. Much overdue time to think.

"Okay, I will call you later then," he leaned in and kissed my cheek.

A cheek kiss? That wasn't a good sign but what did I expect?

**

Since Adam was doing better and better each day, I decided to use my alone time to do some early spring cleaning.

I started cleaning out the closets and made my way into the
kitchen and cleaned out and donated all those unwanted items in
the unused cabinet drawers. Then I put into my donation box old
bedspreads and knick-knacks. It felt good to be purging out all this
outdated stuff. I tossed old candles, magazines, toothbrushes, a few
old toys, and other useless items. Each room I finished, made me
feel like I had made a huge accomplishment. Once I got to my
closet, things became a little more difficult. I associated some of my
old outdated clothes with Thomas. But once I put the first item in
the donation bag, it got easier. I had read a book in the hospital
about cleaning out your belongings called "The Life Changing
Magic of Tidying Up" by Marie Kondo. So, I held each item from
my closet close to me, and if it didn't bring me that spark of joy, I
tossed it in the bag. I found that the clothing that reminded me of
Thomas, actually made me sad. They had to go. Maybe I found the
path to start letting go of Thomas' memory and the self-imposed
ties that held me down. Then I found Thomas' fedora in the way
back of the closet. I remembered him wearing that thinking he was
so cool and me laughing at him as he paraded around in it. I held
the hat in my arms and cried. Ash jumped up licking my face,
somehow trying to comfort me in his own dog way.

I finally finished the closet and felt a great sense of
accomplishment. I had done the whole house in just three days. I
was standing upstairs getting ready to call the Rescue Mission
Thrift Store to come pick up my donations when I looked up and
saw the small set of steps that led up to the attic.

I groaned because I knew what was up there. Thomas' things.
Adam had cleared them out of my room when he was only 14. I
wasn't home when he did it because he knew they didn't belong
there any longer and I couldn't do it myself. I had my bedroom

filled with Thomas' belongings. He had packed everything up and took them up into our small attic.

When I got home and saw my clean empty room, I had yelled at him. I was so angry. I felt violated. But later I realized he was right, and I apologized. My room felt lighter and more peaceful without all those old things in there. They had been up in the attic ever since. I couldn't believe that was eight years ago.

I went into the kitchen and made myself a turkey and swiss sandwich and a glass of tea. I needed to refuel if I was to dare tackle that. I had no idea how I was going to handle it emotionally.

I ate outside on the deck. The days were beginning to be warm enough to be outside with just a jacket on. I ate my sandwich, while I watched the chickadees and sparrows eating from the bird feeder that Collin had put up for me back in early December. Ash sat at my feet giving me puppy eyes, hoping for a handout, as usual.

After I finished up eating, I went back inside, and my phone was ringing. It was Collin calling to check in on me. We made some small talk. The conversation was strained. He sounded sad. And I didn't know how to feel. I hadn't seen him in 6 days. I missed him, but I still wasn't ready. After we hung up, Ash and I headed upstairs and climbed the steps to the attic.

Chapter 22

⟨ঙঙ⟩

The attic was dark and dusty. I found the pull switch to the overhead light, and the bulb gave everything a harsh yellow glow. Ash sneezed from the dust. I looked around at the boxes and other stuff lying around up there. It was overwhelming. I had forgotten how much stuff Thomas had. There were boxes and boxes of papers and files. Boxes of clothing. A long black Burberry umbrella. I still could remember how it felt for us to be walking the streets of Boston, arm in arm, in the rain with him holding it over the two of us. I saw his guitar. He hadn't played it since college. A red toolbox. Several fishing rods. His box of collectible baseball cards and his baseball bat. There was also boxes of toys and stuffed animals from the boys' childhoods. 2 child-sized bright blue bicycles with yellow lightning bolts on the sides. Some boxes held a lot of old books that I had from college too. In the corner was an artificial tree that Thomas and I had bought from a yard sale the summer before our first Christmas together. We didn't have a lot of money when we first got married, and Thomas being the planner that he was, said that the $3 plastic tree would be useful if we couldn't afford to buy a live tree that year. Always planning ahead. He turned out to be right. We used that tree until Adam was born. Decorating with lights and ornaments that had been yard sale finds too. But we loved that tree. I called it our own Charlie Brown Christmas tree.

I walked over and touched the tree. A bristle broke off and then more rained down to the floor. Just like Charlie Brown's tree, I thought. It was dry rotted. It made that decision easier. I lifted it up and carried down the steps, leaving a trail of plastic evergreen needles.

When I got back up there, I walked over to the box with the boys' old toys in it. I picked up a large stuffed cookie monster that was laying on the top and hugged it. It was Adam's. He slept with it every night when he was a toddler. The push button that made him say "me like cookies" was long worn down and didn't even gurgle when I tried it. I pulled out a GI Joe out of the box, Blake's favorite toy. He took it everywhere with him. One day we lost it in the grocery store. He screamed and cried bloody murder. I ran around the store to every place we had been and finally found him mixed in with the bananas on the produce stand. So many memories tied up in this box of forgotten toys. My heart ached. I yearned to be able to go back in time and visit those small moments again. Little boys running down the hall leaving muddy footprints. Sword fighting with paper towel rolls. Peanut butter sandwiches and chocolate milk. Oh, how I missed those days.

I looked through the box at the loose hot wheels, dinosaurs, robots, and nerf guns. I decided not to get rid of any of it. They may want some of these for their children to play with one day, at least that was my excuse.

I repacked the box and moved it off to the side. I worked my way over to my box of books. I grunted. Why I had saved these, I had no idea. All of my old college textbooks were in here. I was just about to take the box downstairs for donation when a sparkly blue notebook caught my eye. My diary!

I pulled it out and opened it in right in the middle.

December 10, 1991

Dear Diary,

Finals are coming, and I am not ready. Guess it will be a long week. Mary Masterson has been vying for the position of editor at the paper here at school, but I'm pretty sure they're giving it to me. She hates me for some reason, and I don't know why. I can tell when I walk in the room and she glares at me like I have done her wrong. I don't know what the heck her major hold up is. But I'm super happy that I will be the editor and not her. I don't think I could work under her.

Today I watched Barbara Walters on The Today Show. She's so amazing. I hope one day, I will be just like her.

***

I flipped the pages of the diary forward and opened up to:

***

February 15, 1993

Dear Diary,

I can't believe Thomas, and I have been dating for three whole months now! We are going tonight to see Phish in concert at Memorial Hall right here on campus! I am thinking of wearing my lace mini skirt and jean jacket. I want to look cute for him.

I went to the mall today and bought a pair of high top converse tennis shoes in pink! They will look so good with my outfit. Maybe I'll even wear my striped pink and white leg warmers. They're still in style enough to be cute!

I won't forget to wear my colored stacked bracelets!
Okay Diary, I gotta go! TTYL

***

I flipped forward a few more pages, anxious to read more of what I wrote about Thomas.

***

March 22, 1993
Dear Diary,

I am certain that I am in love with Thomas Avery. He is so sweet to me, and I know he loves me too. He tells me all the time. I am the envy of the school. Every girl wants to be with Thomas, and he chose me. HE CHOSE ME!

Last night we had sex for the first time. It was awkward but beautiful at the same time. He was as nervous as I was. We were in the back seat of his Toyota Cressida, and he was so gentle and sweet.

I know my parents wouldn't approve of Thomas. I haven't even told them about him yet. I am dreading hearing their lecture. He's not their kind. But Thomas has plans. He's going to open his own firm one day. I don't care what they're going to think because they don't get to choose. I do.

Well, I gotta go do homework because Thomas is coming to get me and we are going to the movies. We are going to see the new Bridget Fonda movie "Point of No Return."

Talk tomorrow! Xoxo!

***

I sat on the floor of my attic reminiscing about those days. Reading my diary was bringing back so many memories. Thomas and I were so young then.

I flipped forward again.

***

May 12, 1994
Dear Diary,

Today Thomas proposed! And I said YES! I cannot wait to be Mrs. Avery! I called my mom, and she was furious. This was the first time I had even told her I had a boyfriend and now he was my fiancé. She was so mad; I almost think they might disown me!

My brother James, called me right after I hung up with her, and he yelled at me too. What are they in some kind of club? Just because both of my brothers married millionaire's daughters, didn't mean I had to marry a child of a millionaire. I was marrying for love, and that was all I cared about.

I just wish Thomas would talk to me about his life before me. He won't talk about his childhood at all. It must have been pretty bad. He says I'm the only good thing that he's ever had in his life. I tell him he's all I ever wanted. I'm not sure he believes me. He tells me he doesn't see what a beautiful rich girl like me could ever see in him.

He's crazy! He's my dream come true, and I would follow him to the end of the earth and back!

I am the happiest girl on earth!

Thank you diary for always listening to me!

XOXO
Sarah

***

I had forgotten how insecure Thomas used to be. That instantly made me sad. He never felt worthy of my love. No matter what I ever did or said would convince him otherwise. He gave all of himself to our family. How could he not see his worth?

I stretched. My back was beginning to ache from sitting on the floor. Ash was starting to whine too. I needed to take him for a walk and give myself a break. I went downstairs to the kitchen and looked at the clock. 5pm.

Had 4 hours already passed?

I put Ash's leash on and took him outside to walk. We were definitely getting an early Spring. The days were warm but the nights were still pretty cold. The trees were all still bare though. I longed for the green to return. I always felt more like myself when there was green around me. I thought about my beautiful flower garden. I looked forward to working in it again. I wondered when I should plant my seeds from Collin. I took a deep breath and waved at my neighbor, Cecilia Harris, as she drove by in her silver Cadillac. She was a crazy eccentric lady but a really nice person. I liked her a lot.

After Ash did his business, we went back inside. I grabbed a bottle of Red Zinfandel and a glass. I took it with me back up to the attic. I was ready to tackle some more boxes.

I took the rest of my books downstairs. When I got back up, I looked at the boxes of Thomas' clothes. I walked over and pulled out a shirt and sniffed it. It smelled stale and old. It had lost the smell of Thomas long ago. My heart was in my throat, but I took each of the boxes of clothes downstairs and put them with the rest of the donations. Adam may want to go through Thomas' clothes to grab some of the t-shirts, but I wasn't going to do it. It was just too painful, and all traces of Thomas were gone from them. There was nothing in the boxes but painful memories.

I got back up to the attic, opened the bottle of wine and poured myself a glass. I sipped on it as I finished sorting the rest of the boxes and took more items downstairs for donation.

All that was left for me to go through were the boxes of papers and documents. I had the thought of throwing them all away. I obviously hadn't needed anything inside of them for years.

I lifted the first box and started to walk down with it, and I remembered Collin's words.

"I would just think it was a strange coincidence that a man of his age would go suddenly up his life insurance policy to provide for his wife for a lifetime, right before he conveniently died"

And I stopped in my tracks. Maybe I should just look through these papers. Maybe there would be some answers, or maybe there would be nothing at all. But it certainly warranted a look through.

The first box was filled with receipts and paperwork for old appliances that I didn't have anymore. There was an old cell phone in there. It was huge! I didn't remember cell phones being that big.

I pushed that box to the side and opened the next one. It was filled with files of his old client's information. I found the same in the next two boxes. Files upon files.

This was starting to get old, and I was getting sore again. I stood up and stretched. Then I sat back down and poured another glass of wine. I sat there drinking it wondering if I should keep looking or not. Ash looked up at me and cocked his head to the side. Why were puppies so cute when they did that? I patted his soft head.

I pulled the final box toward me and opened it. It was Thomas' personal things from his office. I had never looked inside of this box before. Neil had brought it over a few weeks after the memorial service. I was still in the phase of not getting dressed or leaving the house. I didn't answer the door when he knocked. After he left, I found the box sitting outside the front door. I brought it inside and never looked at it again. Somehow it had made its way all the way from Marblehead, Massachusetts, to here in my attic in Wilmington, sitting untouched for 14 plus years.

I peered inside. There was a hole puncher, a stapler and a handful of pens. A framed photo of the boys and me on the beach by my parent's house. I picked it up and held it to my chest. I sat it down on the floor next to me and kept going. I found a few hand-drawn cards and pictures from the boys. A certificate from Blake that he had made in Pre-School that read "this is to certify your title as best dad in the world" I felt tears burning my eyes, but I held them back. I kept digging. A handful of loose paper clips were scattered throughout. There was a ledger inside with his business expenses listed. He was always thorough with what he could claim as a business expense or not. As I dug down, I found a bunch of handwritten phone messages.

There were several messages written on pink paper that read Important Messages in bold with the drawing of an old style corded phone at the top:

Harry Reid called. He says to call him ASAP; He's got a question about his account. He doesn't sound happy. His number is 617-555-9100

Sarah called and wanted you to pick up the boys today.

Neil called and said he wouldn't be in until 3 pm today.

Your insurance agent called and said he is very concerned about the increase in policy limits and he wants you to call him asap. His number is 617-555-8756

My blood ran cold. Why was his insurance agent not happy about the policy changes? He had known Thomas ever since we moved to Boston. He knew Thomas was a planner, so why would this concern him? I mean, we were in the process of buying a second home. Wouldn't he know that Thomas would want to make sure all of his expenses were covered? But 2.5 million was a lot of money for anyone, even counting the houses. They were only $575,000 between the 2 of them. But still....

I kept digging, but I kept the message from the insurance agent out. I wanted to mull over that some more.

At the bottom of the box, I found an old laptop and some crumpled up loose sticky notes.

On one yellow sticky note was Thomas' handwriting.

"Protect my family at all costs."

What did that mean? My heart was pounding so hard, I could hear it in my ears.

I pulled out the laptop and cord. I looked for an outlet and plugged it in. It was large and heavy. I wondered if it would even turn on. I was surprised when I heard the churning of the motor spinning on the inside. Soon Windows XP came up on the screen. It was definitely turning on. It went black for a moment, and I gasped, but then suddenly Thomas' wallpaper came up. It was a photo of the two of us. We were standing next to a tree in our front yard. I couldn't even remember who had taken the photo. We looked so happy in that picture. It was sweet that he had it as his wallpaper. I didn't know. This was the computer that he kept at work. I sat looking at the screen for a few moments. Trying to remember how to search computers for things. I remembered Betsey had helped me check Adam and Blake's computer when they were teenagers. I had not installed any parental controls on it, and she insisted that we check it. I learned that day how to navigate the system somewhat.

I clicked on the Windows Explorer icon, and it pulled up documents and photos. I read through the documents and didn't see much of anything to raise an eyebrow at. He barely had any photos on there. A few that he had emailed himself from our computer of the boys and of me. From our vacations or holidays.

I clicked on the search history. What I saw took my breath instantly. Suddenly the room began to spin, and I knocked over my glass of wine. Ash came over and started licking it up. I yelled no at him and picked him up. I carried him with me as I walked downstairs to the linen closet. I couldn't feel anything. I was numb from head to toe. I grabbed a towel and headed back upstairs. Did I really see what I think I just saw? I put Ash down on the ground and bent over to wipe up the spilled wine. I sat down on the floor. I felt like I was going to vomit. The laptop faced away from me. I reached slowly and turned it around to face me again. There under the Search history heading were the keywords that Thomas had been entering right before our trip. The dates were there going back for weeks. The search terms in front of me were: Accidental Death, what does drowning feel like, life insurance policies and drowning, life insurance investigations after a person's death, Strong currents and tides in the Caribbean Sea, deaths from drowning in Mexico, and the search items went on just like that. My head was throbbing. Why was Thomas searching for information on drowning and life insurance payouts?

I began to sweat. Oh my god....... What had he done? This couldn't be. It must be a coincidence. Why? Oh my god, why? Why would he be searching for these things!? I didn't understand. I felt my head spinning again violently. I stumbled down the steps and threw up in the toilet. I sat there hovering over the toilet with the smell of rancid red wine and vomit coming up my nose, but I couldn't move. I began to sob. What did he do, oh my god, what did he do? I had to find out.

I washed my face and went to find my phone.

I searched under my contacts and found him pretty quickly. Neil Stetson.

I didn't even look at the time. I pushed dial, and the line began to ring.

Chapter 23

⟨ꞋꞋ⟩

$\mathcal{I}$t was the second day after I had woken up from my coma. I stretched out in my uncomfortable hospital bed. My body still ached from my injuries, and I didn't sleep well last night. I humorously thought my body must have gotten enough rest sleeping for six weeks straight. What little sleep I had gotten was filled with bizarre dreams.

I looked around at all the cards and some leftover wilted flowers that decorated my room. There was even a nearly deflated Get Well Soon balloon. So many people had reached out to me. It actually made me feel pretty damn good about myself. Emily had brought over each card and showed them to me yesterday. There were cards from professors at the university, co-workers from the Social Services office, and even some from some of the kids we had worked with recently. I had also gotten a plant from my grandparents on my mother's side. I barely knew them. We had seen them a few times before my dad died, but my mom avoided them after his death. I was actually surprised they even sent the plant. Blake and I had received yearly birthday cards from them with a token cash gift, but other than that, there was virtually no relationship.

The orderlies came in smiling and left a tray of cardboard-flavored eggs and toast for me on my roll-up table for one. I drank the orange juice and loaded the eggs down with ketchup, trying to give them some flavor. Still, they were no good. What I wouldn't give for one of the world-famous omelets from Rosie's Diner. They had the best breakfasts in town bar none! My mouth watered thinking of their Bavarian waffles with hand churned butter and maple syrup. Making the breakfast in front of me even less appetizing.

There was a light tap at the door. The door opened slowly, and Emily peeked her head in.

"Hi there, handsome! I was hoping you would be awake so I could see you before school."

My heart skipped a beat. She looked so beautiful. She was wearing a yellow polo cable knit sweater and blue jeans. Her hair was pulled back into a ponytail. And that smile. That's was enough in and of itself.

She came over and kissed me.

"Wow your breakfast looks a-amazing!" she said laughing.

"Want me to go out really quick, and grab you something decent to eat?"

She had been so sweet to me these past two days. The old Emily was back, and I was happy! Mom had also told me she was here with me every night through this whole thing. I felt so grateful for that. I couldn't imagine how afraid she must have been watching me in the coma night after night. Knowing that she had been here though, brought me a great sense of peace.

"No thanks," I said sheepishly.

I had tried to remember exactly what had happened. My thoughts were pretty fuzzy about the night of the accident. I did remember that she broke up with me, it was Christmas and that I left mom's house pretty angry. I was driving too fast, I know and then.... that's it. No memories until I woke up here and saw my mom standing over me.

"Did you sleep well last night?" she touched my cheek with her fingertips

"Not really..." I yawned.

"I guess your body decided you had enough rest, huh?" she winked.

"I was just thinking that too!" I laughed. We used to do always do that before. Be thinking the same things, at the same times.

She turned on the tv, and we watched the morning news. She scooted her chair right up next to the bed and held my hand.

We watched the news, but my eyes were on her. I couldn't help but stare. It was almost like I was seeing Emily for the first time. I mean, like really seeing her.

After a while, she looked at her watch and got ready to leave. She sighed.

"I don't want to go..." She gave me a cute pouty face.

"Can I get you anything before I leave?"

I looked at her intently.

"Emily? Are we okay?"

She came over to the bed. She smelled so good, like a fresh summer breeze and flowers.

"We are more than okay!" she squeezed my hand, and I saw that she had tears in her eyes.

She leaned over and kissed my cheek. I pulled her in and kissed her hard. She pulled back so she could see my face, and smiled. Then she kissed me again.

After she left, I poked at the now cold cardboard eggs and took a bite of the toast. I almost gagged. Yeah, I wasn't going to eat that.

Three days later I was released to go home. I still had some days of physical therapy ahead, since I hadn't moved my body on my own in weeks, but I was gaining my strength quickly. I was already walking with a cane. It helped that I had some physical therapy while I was still in the coma. Emily told me that the physical therapy guy had come in every day to move my arms and legs.

Mom and Emily both came to escort me home. They put me in a wheelchair to take me out front to where the car was waiting. I felt like a prisoner being let out on parole. When the sunlight hit my face for the first time in almost seven weeks, I had to close my eyes. It blinded me, but it felt amazing. I was truly happy. I sat with my face toward the sun and enjoyed its warmth. The temperature outside was already feeling like Spring.

Emily drove us back to the apartment, and we went inside. As soon as I got in the door, Sasha came running out straight toward me, almost as if she was waiting for me to arrive. She was meowing and rubbing against my legs. I looked at Emily questioning my visitor.

"Oh, Sasha and I thought we would stay here with you for a while to take care of you. *If* that's okay with you?" she looked a little uncertain.

I looked at the cat and back at Emily.

"I was hoping you would say that." I smiled at her.

She smiled so big, and Mom was smiling too. Then they looked at each other and smiled even bigger. I wondered if they had conspired on this together. But, I was actually glad to have them all here. Well, almost glad to have them *all*. But after all, the cat was part of the Emily package deal, and I sure liked the package.

I spent the next few weeks going to physical therapy, reading and working extra hours at the Social Services office. I had missed the beginning of the Spring semester, so school was over for me for this semester. I would have to work through the summer to catch up. I didn't mind though. In the past, I would have been pretty bent about getting off of "the plan", but somehow, the accident had changed me. The way I had always done things before, seemed foolish now. The restless spirit inside me had calmed, and my need to control every single aspect of my life had quelled inside of me. I wanted to enjoy this second chance at life. It was a gift, and I wanted to appreciate every moment.

One day I was over at Mom's house, and she was cooking for me. It was just her and me. Collin wasn't there, and Emily was off studying. I was overcome with guilt over feeling so resentful toward her these last few years. I had been so angry and prideful. All she had done was need me. It wasn't wrong of her to need me. I was the only thing she had in this world that she could rely on. And I punished her for it. I walked up to her, and she turned around and faced me.

"Mom, I'm so sorry..." I was holding back tears.

"Oh, my gosh, Adam, for what?"

"I have been a real jerk, and I'm sorry."

"Oh honey, you haven't been a jerk at all. You've been a wonderful son, and I appreciate you."

How could she be so compassionate?

I put my arms around her, and she held me tight. I started to cry; I couldn't hold back the tears any longer.

Emily and I spent so much time together, and things were different for us now. Our dynamic was better than ever. And we talked a lot more than we used to. Really talked. I felt more at ease with her. She had changed too. She had an ease about her that was contagious. We laughed a lot more and actually got out and did more things together. Before the accident, I was too busy to make time to take her on real dates, but now with my attitude shift, I found I had more time than I realized and took advantage of it. We played mini golf, ate pizza out, and played Frisbee on the beach. We even went to the park once just to swing on the swings. Emily squealed with joy when she was swinging. I loved her laugh more than anything else on the planet. I felt so guilty about the way I had treated her before. Especially that last night we were together when I was so enamored by Becca. Emily blew Becca out of the water in every department. I can't believe it took me until now to see that.

One Saturday I found myself at the mall standing in front of a big chain jewelry store. I went in and came out with a simple ¼ carat pear-shaped diamond engagement ring, haloed with a ring of miniature diamonds. It was rare and unique, just like Emily. I didn't plan on buying a ring that day. I had actually gone to the mall to buy a new pair of running shoes. There was a Foot Locker there, and I had my eyes on the new Nike Pegasus. I was walking through the food court to find my way to the shoe store when an elderly couple caught my eye. The man had walked up to his table with a giant cookie and gave it to his wife. She laughed with delight, and he kissed her on the top of her head then she took a big bite. I laughed to myself. They were adorable. More than adorable. They were perfect. The strange thing was that they reminded me of Emily and me. And I stopped in my tracks stunned because I realized right at that moment that I wanted to spend the rest of my life with Emily. We belonged together. That couple would be us in

50 years. What had I been holding back for? She was the one for me. She brought me more joy than I could even imagine. She completed me in ways I didn't know were incomplete in the first place until she was there filling up all my empty places. All the fears that had been holding me back just vanished. I practically ran to the jewelry store. I carried the white velvet box in my pocket for weeks. I didn't know how or when I would propose, but I always kept it with me. I knew I would know when the time was right.

One day I was sitting on the couch when she came in from school. She had a serious look on her face.

"Adam, we need to talk." She walked over and sat down.

My heart began to pound. Was she breaking up with me again? Things were going so well! I didn't understand! If she only knew I had a ring for her.... My mind raced with a million thoughts in the 10 seconds before she began to speak.

"Well, you remember the job in Boulder?" she looked at me intently.

I could feel beads of sweat forming on my forehead. She couldn't leave me. She wouldn't....

"They offered me the job." My heart was breaking, but I kept a poker face while my stomach was twisting up in knots.

She reached out and grabbed my hand.

"But I turned them down," she was still looking at me with such intent.

Relief flooded through my body, and I released the breath I didn't even realize I was holding.

She smiled so sweetly. I loved looking at her face.

"I accepted a position at a small firm here in Wilmington."

I couldn't believe it! My body surged with joy.

"Wilmington?!"

"Yes, I chose Wilmington. Because I cannot imagine my life without you and if Wilmington is where you want to be then that's where I want to be too."

There were tears in her eyes.

"And Adam, I am truly sorry for the way I handled things before the accident. I realize now what is important, and that is you and me. None of the rest matters," She smiled sweetly.

I slid off the couch and got down on my knees in front of her. I pushed her hair away from her face and wiped her tears away.

"Emily, I want you to know that you have always been enough for me. I am sorry that I ever made you feel like you weren't good enough! You are the best person I have ever known, and I am a better person for just knowing you. I love you more than words can say. I am thankful for every day that I get to wake up to your beautiful face. And I'm even starting to love Sasha," although that was tiny bit stretch of the truth, I had grown fonder of the cat.

She giggled and looked over at Sasha who had perched herself at the top of the couch, to get a better view of the happenings.

"Emily?" She looked back at me with dreamy eyes.

"I want to spend the rest of my life with you if you will have me?" I pulled the ring box out of my pocket and held it out to her.

She burst into to tears, and I grew terrified for just a moment until I realized she was laughing too.

"Oh, Adam Avery, you are so full of surprises! I love you so much!" Her face was beaming.

"And yes, YES I will marry you!"

She opened the ring box and gasped.

"Oh, my gosh Adam! If I had my choice of any ring in this whole world, this would be the one I would choose!" she was staring at the ring in the awe. I was so happy that she liked it.

183

I took the ring out of the box and placed it on her finger. It fit. I sighed with relief.

She threw herself down on top of me, and we made love right there on the living room floor. Afterwards, we laid together on the floor, and she cuddled up next to me. I put my arm around her and kissed the top of her head. I had never felt so sure about anything, or so happy, in my whole life.

Chapter 24

My flight touched down at Boston's Logan International Airport at 12:40 pm.

I got up to grab my bag, feeling the strain of not sleeping much last night. I had rested my eyes a little during the layover in New York, but it hadn't helped at all. I walked out of the airport and hailed a cab. I had the guy take me to The Hyatt Regency hotel. I had an eerie sense of Deja-vu when I walked in. I had lost my fondness for hotel lobbies.

I hadn't called ahead, so I hoped they had a room available. A curly haired blonde greeted me with a smile when I reached the front desk.

She was able to book a room for me with an early check-in. I went up to the room without the bellhop. I only had one carry-on bag and my purse, I didn't need his help. Plus, I wanted to go up alone. I had so much on my mind. I got inside the room and set down my bags. I walked over and looked out the window of my River View room. Boston. My hometown. It felt like a hundred years had passed since the last time I was here. The Charles River flowed just the same as it had before. The historic buildings still stood tall with their ornate architecture. There was an undeniable charm about this city, but despite the nostalgia, I still felt out of place. Wilmington had become my home.

I sat on the edge of the bed and looked at my watch. It was 1:30 pm. It was time to call Neil and see if he was ready for a visit.

He picked up on the first ring.

"Sarah? I was wondering when you were going to call? I don't have any afternoon classes if you want to talk now?"

"Well, actually Neil, I was hoping to see you in person to talk."

"What? I mean, sure...okay, when were you thinking of coming to town?" he seemed nervous.

"I am here now," I stated matter of fact.

"What do you mean here now?' I could hear the shock in his voice.

"I mean, I am here in Boston, and I would like to come see you as soon as possible."

I had kept my emotions in check, but now I felt my walls crumbling, and I had to hold back my tears.

"Wow, you're really here? Okay then, I'm still at school, but I can meet you in about an hour. How about Pappa's Place? Do you remember where that is?"

I remembered it alright. It was a place that we had went with Neil and his wife on numerous double dates. It was a favorite. I honestly wished he hadn't chosen that place.

"Okay, I'll leave here now, and I will see you soon."

I went into the bathroom to freshen up. I looked in the mirror. I had bags under my eyes from lack of sleep and looked ten years older. I ran a brush through my hair and splashed cold water on my face. That was as good as it was going to get today.

I was able to get a cab pretty quickly because one pulled up just as I walked out the front door. Depositing a woman wearing a full-length fur coat, a giant black hat, and gloves. She had a tiny white poodle on a leash. I almost laughed. I had forgotten the eccentricities of big cities.

We drove down the streets passing Granary Burial Ground, Kings Chapel, and Old South Meeting House. All landmarks that had been here long before I was born. There were a lot of new things to see too. It is strange how much things can change, yet seem exactly the same.

The cab pulled up in front of Pappa's. I sat for a moment while the pain welled up inside of me. The last time I was here, I was with Thomas. We had walked here hand in hand after going to The Harrison-Genneau Art Gallery together. He had kissed me right before we stepped inside the door.

"Hey lady, is this where you wanted to go?" the cab driver had turned around in his seat and was looking at me.

"Oh yes, I'm sorry," my face flushed with embarrassment. I paid the fare and stepped out of the cab onto the busy sidewalk. People hustled by, pushing and shoving to get through. Another thing I forgot about big cities. Everyone was always in a rush. I walked inside Pappa's, and it was exactly the same. Nothing had changed in 14 years. I felt a lump rise up in my throat.

I looked around for Neil and didn't see him. A chubby, bald man that I didn't know was waving at me. I wondered if this was some new way of picking up women? I quickly turned away from his gaze. He got up from his table and came over to me.

"Sarah!"

It was Neil! I was in shock. I hadn't recognized him at all. The last time I saw Neil, he had a head full of hair and was quite a bit leaner.

"Hi, Neil." I tried not to act surprised at his appearance.

"Thank you for seeing me!" I faked my best smile.

He reached in and hugged me.

"Sarah, you look wonderful. As beautiful as ever!" I wondered if he could see what I saw in the mirror just a bit ago. He took my arm and led me over to his table

We sat down, and the waiter came straight over and got our drink orders. I ordered an espresso and water, and Neil ordered whiskey.

When the waiter walked away, Neil looked at me with a serious expression.

"Sarah, I've been expecting your call for quite some time." He looked at me intently.

"Thomas said that you would call. But it certainly took longer than I expected it to."

I looked at him with complete bewilderment. What did he mean, Thomas said I would call?

"What do you mean, Neil? Why did Thomas think I would call!?"

"Thomas knew that you were a smart woman. That one day you would put two and two together about everything. And you would have lots of questions."

That statement left me with a massive sense of uneasiness. I thought of my discovery from last night, and my heart sank.

"Neil, I found his laptop last night. I hadn't looked in the box of work stuff that you left before I moved to North Carolina. It sat up in the attic for years. I was doing some spring cleaning and found the box."

"What did you find out?" Neil looked at me sympathetically.

"I went to his search history and found out that he was looking for information on the internet about accidental drowning and insurance claims..." my voice cracked, and my hands began to shake.

Neil nodded his head.

"Sarah, If I had known he was serious about it, I would've stopped him, I would've told you, but I didn't think he'd actually do it." Neil's face grimaced with deep-seated guilt.

"Oh my god.... what do you mean?" my heart was pounding in my ears.

The waiter came and delivered our drinks. I didn't need the espresso anymore.

Neil took a long sip of his Jack and Coke.

"Thomas came to me a few weeks before he died, and he told me that if anything were to happen to him and you called, to give you this key."

He pulled a key out of his pocket and laid it on the table in front of me.

I looked at it like it was a snake ready to strike.

"Why did Thomas think something could happen to him?" I pushed for more information.

Neil rubbed his forehead.

"Thomas made some bad investments back in the day. He was pretty distraught over it. His clients all trusted him, and he had made some big promises about payouts. Most of them had given over big chunks of their life savings. Thomas always had a knack for knowing where to invest, but this time he was wrong, and he was wrong in a *big* way. He was desperate to make it right. He was hiding what had happened from everyone, even me. I found out about it by accident. I saw the spreadsheet open on his laptop. He walked in, and when I looked at him, he started to cry. A grown man, crying. Thomas, no less. By the time I found out, Thomas had already gone to some loan sharks, to fund his client's accounts, back to what they were before the bad investments. It was a hefty sum of money. In fact, the debt that you paid after Thomas died, mostly went to those people. The problem was that Thomas had borrowed more than he needed because he felt sure that he could play the market and make enough money to pay back the loan sharks and have some extra money to give to the clients. He was happy for a while thinking he had figured it all out. Unfortunately, that didn't work out for him either. He was on an unlucky streak and made some terrible investments. I think the stress was clouding his mind. He lost everything, including you guys' savings. He cashed out all of his bonds and IRA's to give some money to the men he had borrowed from, to try to buy himself some time. But even with all that, it didn't put a dent in what he owed. And they wanted their money. They started showing up at the office and then showing up at random places Thomas went other than work. These were some bad men, Sarah. These are not the kind of men that you just don't pay back. They wanted their money, and Thomas didn't have it. Toward the end, Thomas had gotten so desperate that he even went to your dad and asked for help. He knew your dad had the money and well, your dad, he flat out refused. He laughed at Thomas and told him 'Now Sarah will see what kind of man you really are.' Thomas was pretty devastated."

He went to my dad? I couldn't believe it. How could I have not known? I felt a darkness growing inside of me.

Neil shifted in his seat.

"The loan sharks were starting to rough him up. They threatened him repeatedly; they threatened to hurt you and the boys. That's when Thomas started talking to me about accidental death and insurance. He joked that he was worth more dead than alive. I had no idea at the time that he wasn't joking. It wasn't long after that he came to me and told me to give you the key if anything happened. He said you'd figure it all out one day. I just assumed that he meant if the loan sharks were to hurt him or something. I didn't know what to do. I didn't have the money to help get him out of this either. Honestly, I was terrified for myself and my family. I justified it in my mind, that loan sharks didn't really kill people over loans like they did in the movies. I just figured that they were trying to scare Thomas. After Thomas' death, I was even more afraid of them. They kept showing up at the office, even after they were paid. It was like they had a vendetta against Thomas. That's why I closed the company and went to teaching. I didn't want to be anywhere near those men."

Neil's hands were shaking, and sweat was forming on the top of his bald head. I couldn't speak. My heart was in my throat.

"Sarah, if I had known, I would've tried to help him more. I just didn't know how bad it was until it was too late," Neil's eyes were unfocused, lost in memory.

"Too late?" I asked.

"One day we came into the office, and the whole place was a mess. They had done a real number on it. The desks and chairs were turned over. Papers were thrown everywhere, and there was a note on Thomas' office door. It said, 'your family is next.'"

The waiter came to take our order. Neil put up his hand and asked him to give us more time.

"It was the next week that you guys went on your trip to Cancun." Neil was looking down at the drink in his hands. His hands were stubby and worn with age.

My body began to tremble.

I thought back to how Thomas had surprised me with the trip. We had been talking about it for months, and he kept promising me after this big deal at work went through, he would take me to celebrate. I assumed it had succeeded. I hadn't even questioned the timing.

Neil's face was contorted trying to hold back tears.

"If I had known he was really going to hurt himself...." he didn't finish his sentence before I spoke up.

"But he didn't Neil! He drowned! It was an accident! Thomas would never really kill himself! He wouldn't leave me and the boys like that!" My face was burning with anger.

Neil's face was red and tears were streaming down his chubby cheeks.

"Neil, he was joking when he told you that...."

He didn't look like he believed me.

I reached across the table and touched his hand. I hated him right now for not helping Thomas, but I couldn't blame him either. Because I didn't know what was going on, and I was married to him. I knew he went through that bad phase, but then everything turned around. Although, I did remember there was a day Thomas had come home with a busted lip and black eye. When I asked him about it, he had said that he fell off the treadmill at the gym and busted up his face pretty good. It never crossed my mind that he could have been lying. That must have been related to what Neil is telling me.

I picked up the key; it was a small bronze key with the number 99864 on it.

"Neil, what does this key go to?"

"It's a safety deposit box at Boston Savings and Loan. Your name is on file there. All you will have to do is show them your ID, and they'll take you to the box."

I immediately stood up.

"Neil, I have to go now."

He looked so downtrodden. Apparently, talking to me had not relieved any of the guilt he was carrying.

"Sarah, I'm so sorry," a small sob came out.

I went around the table, and he stood up. I hugged him, and he sobbed again.

I walked out of the restaurant. My hands were still shaking. I had to get to that safety deposit box. What had Thomas put in there? I was filled with so many emotions. Fear, anger, guilt. How could I have not known my husband was suffering so severely? My heart anguished, as a cab pulled up.

"Boston Savings and Loan, please," I told the cab driver.

Within 12 minutes I was standing inside the lobby of the historic Boston Savings and Loan. The floors were made of marble, and the ceilings were 30 feet tall. My shoes echoed on the floors as I walked up to the teller's booth. She directed me over to customer relations. When I got there, no one was at the desk, so I sat in an oversized red leather chair in the small waiting area.

Finally, an older woman with her hair in a tight bun came to the desk and sat down. I told her I was there to open up a safety deposit box. She nodded at me with narrowed eyes. She kept looking over at me and eying my clothes. I knew I was a disheveled mess. I tried to straighten my shirt but gave up quickly. She picked up her phone and called someone on the phone to come over and get me.

After about ten long agonizing minutes. A young man, around Adam's age, came and got me. He had red hair and light freckles. An all-American look. He led me down a hallway into a large room filled with metal drawers of different sizes. They almost looked like post office boxes. He asked me to wait, and he went down the corridor and disappeared. He quickly reappeared with the box for me.

"Do you have your key?" he had a soft-spoken way about him and an accent I couldn't place. He was definitely not from Boston.

I nodded.

He set the box down on a large table in front of me. It was counter height, so I was able to stand up to open the box.

He pulled out his key, and I withdrew the key that Neil had given me. He put him inside the first keyhole. My hands were shaking so terribly that it took several tries to get mine inside of the second keyhole. We turned them together, and I heard a click.

"Okay, I will be down the hall, if you need anything," he smiled.

He walked off, and I stared at the metal box in front of me. I tried to picture Thomas here, placing something inside of this box for me. I couldn't imagine what it could be. My anxiety to rush and open it waged war with my fear of what I would find inside. Finally, I lifted the metal lid slowly. I peered inside, and there was an envelope. Nothing else. I picked up the envelope. On the outside of it in Thomas' handwriting was written: "To my beautiful Sarah."

I opened the envelope and pulled out a handwritten letter.

My dear Sarah,

If you are reading this, then I am gone. My heart is so full of heaviness that I can barely write this letter to you. I think of our early days together and how happy and free we used to be. Not a worry in the world, our whole future in front of us. What I wouldn't give to be back there again. Our love is a love that only comes once in a lifetime. I have been so lucky to call you my wife, my love, my friend. I want you to know that you are the reason that I know love. Before you came into my life, love did not exist to me. And now I know love is the very reason for existence. I look at you and our beautiful boys, and I know now why I was created. I was created to love you all. But with love comes great responsibility. The responsibility to protect. And that's what I must do. I have made some terrible mistakes and now I have to pay for them. It is the only way to keep you and the boys safe.

Please believe me, if there were any other way, I would gladly take it. I have tried every avenue and found only roadblocks. I owe some very bad men a lot of money. I have lost all of our retirement and used all of our savings trying to fix what I did. And I failed. These men want to hurt me, but worst of all, they want to hurt you and the boys. I cannot; I will not allow that to happen. I have upped our life insurance policy to pay these men back and to ensure that you and the boys will be taken care of. I plan to take my life, in order to save yours. I must make it look like an accident because the insurance will not pay out for suicide. After you read this, do not tell anyone what you know, because the insurance company can come back and collect the money from you, after the fact. I know that you are devastated, and I am sorry that I am hurting you by doing this. But this is the only way I know to keep you safe. We can't run, and we can't hide. They have the means to find us no matter where we would go. I want the boys to have a normal life, not a life on the run. And unfortunately, the situation has gotten so bad now, that even if I paid them back, they would still kill me. Either way, I am dead. This way I can protect you and the boys. I hope that one day you will understand why I had to do this. When you get the insurance money, Neil will make sure the men are paid in full. They shouldn't ever bother you. Their grievance is with me, and I will be gone. Getting involved with them was the worst mistake of my life. I was naïve to think that I could do it without serious consequences.

Even if I could find a way to pay them back in full, on my own, they would not let me live. I have crossed the line with them, and they want blood. If they were to find me alive, they would most certainly kill me, possibly putting you and the boys in more danger. This is the only way.

Please believe me, if I could change this, I would. It is too late now, and I have to do what is right to protect you and the boys.

I am thankful though that my last days will be with you and you alone. You are the love I always dreamed of. And wherever I go after I leave this earth know, that I will be waiting for you there. Dreaming of the moment, I will hold you in my arms again. Please forgive me Sarah for the mistakes that I made. But please know that I always loved you and I always will. I wish you a long and happy life. Love extra hard on the boys for me. I will miss them terribly.

Thank you for loving me and for all the wonderful days we had together.

Stay strong my beautiful Sarah.

Love forever,

Your husband, Thomas

I dropped to the floor and began to sob. "Thomas, no!" The reality of what he had done began to sink in.

Pain leeched through every fiber of my body. I could barely breathe.

"Oh god, Thomas, no!"

"Please....no!"

Chapter 25

I woke up just before dawn. The dark room was unfamiliar and cold. I left the thermostat in the hotel room too low. My sleep was full of fitful tossing and turning. At some point in the night I had a dream that I was standing on a river bank at sundown, and suddenly I saw Thomas drifting away face down, and I tried to call out to him and slipped down the muddy bank into the water, but he was gone. I woke up crying around 2 am. I felt so helpless. I got up and poured a glass of water from one of the complimentary bottles of Evian on the counter. I went over and sat down on the windowsill, looking out over the darkened city. Lights were coming from a few of the buildings. Streetlights reflected onto the river. I could hear voices mumbling as they passed my room walking down the hallway. Suddenly, I felt so alone. More alone than I had ever felt. Thomas was really gone. There was no denying it now.

I laid back down around 4 am and fell into a deep sleep at once. Sometime during the hours before dawn, the nightmare came upon me. I was again treading water in the darkness. I looked around and could see nothing but water all around me. No lights, no boats, no people. Alone in the abyss of water. I began to panic; there was no shoreline, no safety net. I was lost and alone here. I panicked and started thrashing around, and the ink like water splashed all around me. Then I realized the water was too wide to swim to shore and there was no way to reach safety. All hope vanquished, I began to sink, slowly into the dark water until I was gone.

When I woke up, I checked the clock. It was 6 am. I couldn't believe I had slept soundly those 2 hours. I rolled over and looked at the spackled ceiling and sighed. I thought back over the dream. Over and over the same dream since childhood. Tormenting my nights. Why wouldn't it let me be?

I got up, packed up my meager belongings, and checked out of the hotel. As I rode in the cab down the familiar, yet now seemingly unfamiliar streets, my tears fell quietly. I thought about how strange it was that a place could change so much in such a short period of time. But then I wondered if it was really me that had changed the most? I asked the driver take me past our old house in Marblehead. He stopped right in front, and I sat staring at it through the cab window. It looked almost the same. The new owners had pulled up the gardenia bushes I had planted and replaced it with monkey grass. And the baby tree that Thomas and I had planted when Adam was 3 was huge now. I guessed now was maybe 25 or 30 feet tall. For a moment, I could see my boys, riding tricycles on the driveway while Thomas and I followed behind. Thomas looking back at me periodically to smile.

The driver turned around and looked at me but didn't say a word. I gave him a nod, and we started in the direction of my parent's house.

We drove down Tamaron Lane under a canopy of huge old oak trees that had been there since I was a little girl. There were mothers pushing strollers and joggers passing on the sidewalks. We finally reached my parent's driveway. The cab driver pulled up to the gates that blocked the entrance and made sure I could reach the intercom.

A voice came crackling out of the worn-out speaker, "Cargill Residence, how may I help you?"

"Please tell Mr. & Mrs. Cargill that their daughter is here to see them."

We waited for what seemed like forever. Then the iron gates began to creak and open. We drove down the driveway and pulled around the circle drive. At the center of the driveway was a fountain with a giant winged cherub but the water was no longer flowing.

I paid the driver, and he helped me get my bag out of the car.

I walked up the brick path to the oversized front door. Before I could ring the bell, Nanny Marie opened it. She had tears in her eyes.

"Oh, Miss Sarah, it's really you!" she came out onto the stoop, threw her arms around me and gave me a big hug.

"How are you, Nanny?" I asked. "It's so good to see you."

I had known Nanny almost my whole life. She was a young woman hired by my mother from a Nanny referral agency. She was just as plump now, as she was when I was a child. Nanny had practically raised me. My mother was always off to her meetings, to play tennis, go to lunch, or a charity event. Much too busy to raise a child. I had such fond memories of Nanny. We had tea parties with my dolls on the lawn every Saturday until I was too big to play pretend anymore. She fed me, bathed me, and loved me with the all the tenderness you could want from a mother.

I was glad to see Nanny again. There was comfort in just being near her.

"Oh, come on in the house sweetheart, you look exhausted!"
She tugged on my arm and pulled me inside.

I stepped inside the foyer that was almost as big as my living
room now. I stood on the marble tiled floor and looked out in front
of me at the curved grand staircase. It had been so long since I stood
in this spot. Just then a man I didn't recognize came forward. He
was tall and lanky with grey hair and a strong jawline.

"Ma'am, may I take your bags to your room?" I thought he
had a slight British accent, but I couldn't be sure.

"No thank you, I won't be staying," I said adamantly.

I looked over at the man with questioning eyes.

"That's Gerald, your parent's butler," Nanny offered.

"What happened to Edmund?" I questioned.

"Oh, darlin' he passed on a few years back," Nanny sniffled.

Tears came to my eyes. I hadn't known. Edmund was one of
my favorite people in the house. He was my personal driver, as well
as another playmate for me. I rode piggyback on him many times. I
wondered now how his knees stood it on this marble floor.
Something I never thought of as a child. To me it was as simple as,
can I ride again? And his answer was always yes. My heart ached at
the thought of him passing. I should have stayed in touch with him
and Nanny better.

"I'm sorry Nanny; I didn't know." I was bitter that my parents
didn't let me know.

"Now don't you worry your pretty little head, he has gone on
to a better place." she smiled at me and gave me another hug.

"What I am thankful for right now, is that you are here in this
house again. It's like a breath of fresh air just washed in!"

I felt shame immediately. If she only knew why I was here.

She whisked off to prepare tea for me, while Gerald showed
me to the drawing room.

Which kind of irritated me, I wasn't a guest.

I sat down on a purple velvet couch. It looked like it was from the Victorian Era. I glanced around the room. All new furniture. That was Mother, redecorating every couple of years. Nothing more to do with her sad life than to spend money.

I had been waiting for over 15 minutes and still no sign of my parents. I was sure they were punishing me for showing up unannounced. Nanny Marie came in with the tea tray and set it on the table in front of me. She prepared my tea, just the way I liked it. Such a good memory, I thought. Sweet, caring Nanny her face was worn with age. I wished she could come live with me, but I knew she wouldn't leave my mother. She was loyal, though I didn't understand why she would be to someone like my mother. She never treated her that well. I am guessing it was because she felt guilty about Nanny raising her children instead of her doing it. But Nanny never held it against her. She always kept a positive, bright attitude.

Nanny went out of the room, and I sipped my tea. Suddenly I was hit with an overwhelming sadness and anger. I thought of Thomas sitting right here, in this same room, getting the same disrespect, I was getting. He had come here for help. I cannot imagine how nervous and humiliated he must have been. I felt tears coming to my eyes, and I willed them back. I would not let them see me cry.

My parents had long ago ostracized me. If you don't do things the Cargill way, you are no longer part of the family. Regardless of blood relation. I made a point to never ask them for one thing after Thomas died. I was determined to make it without them. Although they had volunteered their support for the search reward money when Thomas was first missing. I know that was only done, to prove them right about their opinion, that he had run off. To them, the satisfaction of being right about Thomas would have been worth any price. My mother called me once after I moved to Wilmington. She was in a great mood and said that now that I was rid of "that man" I could come back to living a sensible life. I was so angry that I hung up on her. After that, I never heard from them again. The boys received a yearly birthday card, but that was it. I had picked up the phone to call them on numerous occasions, but I could not bring myself to do it. The way that they had treated Thomas and me when we were together was disturbing, but the way they acted after his death, was unforgivable. The hurt was too deep, and the damage too severe.

I heard the distinct sound of heels clicking on marble, and my mother appeared in the entrance way. She looked much older. Her face contorted with plastic surgery. She was always very vain. I'm sure she was trying everything to retain her youth. She was wearing a long silk purple maxi gown and over it was a full-length floral kimono. She accented it with a long string of white pearls.

"Sarah, my darling daughter!" she said so convincingly, I almost believed she was happy to see me.

"Where is Father?" I asked bluntly.

"Well, not even a kiss for your mother then?" she huffed.

"I need to talk to both of you, actually." My face stayed expressionless.

"I should have known you had an agenda." She turned her head away from me and walked toward the tall wall of arched windows, keeping her back to me. The ceilings in this room were 20 feet tall. I always thought it was designed that way, to make visitors feel smaller.

My father walked silently into the room and just looked at me. His hair was completely white now. He was wearing a black suit and tie. He too had aged but was still as just as handsome as I remembered. I felt sad, but only for a moment, and my resolve returned.

"Sarah, what brings you here?" he asked in a business-like tone, his face was like stone.

When she heard my father's voice, my mother came over and stood by him. I had seen this stance before. Two against one. And again, I thought of poor Thomas.

"Why didn't you help him?" I tried my best to control my voice, but I know it came out coated with hatred.

"Whatever do you mean?" my mother feigned ignorance well.

"Margaret, I will handle this!" My father stepped forward half of a step.

I didn't back up.

"Why didn't you help him!? He is dead because of YOU!" I started to shake.

"No Sarah, he is dead because of himself. If he had any brains, to begin with, he would've never gotten into that mess in the first place. And for the matter, I had no reason to bail him out," He looked at me with a smug smile on his face. I never knew that my parents were capable of evil. I knew they were greedy and prideful, but never thought of them as evil.

Suddenly I was filled with utter rage. I ran toward him and started hitting him on the chest.

"How could you!? I loved him!" I sobbed as I hit him over and over.

Gerald came running into the room and pulled me off. I was kicking and screaming.

My father looked at me emotionlessly, while he brushed off his shirt.

"Well sounds like you made a bad investment too. You can't say we didn't warn you."

He and my mother turned and walked out of the room.

My father turned back around and looked at Gerald.

"Please show her to the door." He didn't even look at me.

I looked over at Nanny, and she was crying.

As soon as my parents disappeared from view, she came running over to me whispering:

"Oh, Miss Sarah, I want you to know that I prayed for that husband of yours. I loved him because you did. And I am so sorry, that he's gone."

I reached over and hugged her tightly.

Gerald had a smug and unfriendly look on his face. Obviously, he took his job seriously.

"Miss, it's time for you to go."

He picked up my bag and carried it to the door.

"Your father's driver, Stephan, will take you wherever you need to go," he said with contempt in his voice.

"No thank you, I will call a cab!" I almost shouted.

I wasn't about to take anything, including a ride from them.

He looked at me with an eerie smile.

"You'll need to leave the premises now. Therefore, not affording you the time to wait for your own form of transportation."

When I stepped outside, a black Lincoln town car was waiting, and the driver came up and took my bag from Gerald. The guy was a short stubby man with dark greased back hair.

He placed my bag in the trunk and then opened the backseat door for me. He didn't make eye contact with me. It was as if he'd already been informed about me.

I got into the car and sat down on the soft, luxurious seat. I was still shaking and crying. The car was black on black on the inside and smelled of leather. It brought back many childhood memories.

I looked out the window and Nanny was standing on the steps wiping her face with a handkerchief. She was waving. No one else was in sight. I half hoped my mother to come running out with regret, but the door did not open.

My flight wasn't for 4 hours, but I had him go ahead and take me to the airport. There was nothing left for me in this city.

***

After returning from Boston, I sank into a depression. I didn't answer calls or texts. I didn't meet Betsey for lunch. I didn't take Ash for walks. I gave Adam excuses for not seeing him and Emily. Collin came by twice, and I sent him away. I lied and told him that I had the flu. He dropped by with flowers and chicken soup, ringing the bell but leaving before I could answer. He left a note saying feel better soon; I miss you.

It was two weeks since the trip to Boston, and my grief over what Thomas had done was consuming me. I finally decided to get out of the house and go for a walk on the beach. Before I knew it, I was driving toward Sunset beach. I wanted to go back to the Kindred Spirit mailbox. I didn't know why.

I got to the beach around 4 pm. It was fairly empty. I walked the 1.4 miles from the pier to the mailbox. When I got there, I walked up and opened the box. There were all new letters inside. A white envelope with gold star stickers all over it caught my eye. I pulled it out. I felt a little guilty for pulling someone's letter out, but really that's what this box is for. To share. I opened it, and on the inside, there was a folded slip of paper. I opened the paper, and the words written on it were "LET GO." I nearly dropped the letter. I looked all around in every direction. Was this letter for me?

My heart was pounding, and I was trembling. I fell to my knees right there by the box and sobbed loudly. I balled up the piece of paper and pounded the sand. I cried until all the strength to cry had left my body. I sat quietly staring out at the ocean.

Let go! The same words from my dream about Thomas. Was Thomas trying to get this message to me? But I didn't know how to be me without Thomas, the memory of Thomas that I have kept alive for so long. I felt so lost. So hopeless. Thomas, my love, my life was gone, what was I going to do?

Then suddenly it occurred to me that I was sitting in a virtual image of my water nightmare. I was figuratively treading water with no sign of the shore in sight. No help for my pain. No escape from the darkness that surrounded me. And I had two choices. I could either save myself or surrender to the abyss, as I did in my nightmare, over and over again. And I did *want* to sink into the abyss, to disappear, to make all of this pain go away.

Seagulls called overhead. And a small crab scurried past me. Off in the distance, I saw a little girl with an older woman. The little girl had white blonde bouncing curly hair and was running on the beach. Occasionally looking back at the woman and was giggling. Then the little girl came running right up to me.

"He-wo," she said in a little toddler voice. With her beautiful round green eyes, she looked directly into my eyes, almost as if she could understand my pain.

The woman came up and said hello to me as well. The little girl was her granddaughter. She told me her husband had passed away a few months ago. She said that she and her granddaughter took daily walks together. It helped keep her focused on what was important. We made a little small talk for a bit and then they walked off hand in hand. At the last moment, before they disappeared out of sight, the little girl turned and looked back at me, waved and then smiled.

At that moment, something clicked inside of me. I realized I did have a future and a life worth living. Even without Thomas. I had my own life to live. And maybe one day, I would be like that woman playing on the beach with a little one again. I didn't need Thomas to make my life okay. I would always miss him, but my life could flourish, and I could be happy. Being with Collin had taught me that I could even love again.

I walked back to the car with hope and a renewed sense of self. Freedom had been awarded to me.

As I drove home, I thought about Collin and the time I had spent with him. I sadly began to realize that everything I had based the relationship with him was only because of Thomas. And it was wrong of me. I had been with Collin for all the wrong reasons. And I had to make it right.

I knew ending the relationship would break his heart, but it was what I had to do. It would break mine too. But all these months of being with Collin was merely me trying to keep Thomas here with me. It was not healthy for me nor fair to Collin.

I picked up my cell phone and dialed his number.

When he picked up, he sounded so happy.

"Sarah, I am so glad that you called!"

"Hi Collin, can you meet me? I need to talk to you." I tried not to let him hear the sadness in my voice. I wanted to explain everything to him in person.

He was silent for just a moment

"Is everything okay?" his voice was unsure.

"I would rather talk to you about it in person if that's okay?"

He was silent.

"Collin?"

"Okay, I'm at my house, come on over." His voice sounded strange and distant.

I pulled down the gravel driveway toward Collin's house, I knew for the last time. I felt sick to my stomach. I pep talked myself. I couldn't keep being selfish. The right thing to do isn't always the easy thing to do. I had to do this. I had to.

His car was there in the driveway, and he was sitting on the porch swing waiting for me.

I got out of my car and walked up onto the porch and sat down with him. The grass was so green, and the aroma of fresh clippings was in the air. He must have just cut it. A warm breeze blew across us, and the birds were singing. The leaves on the trees rustled in the wind. We sat together in silence for a moment listening to the sounds around us, helping us avoid the inevitable. I looked over at Collin. It was almost as if he knew what was coming. I had never seen Collin look as sad as he did at this moment.

He broke the silence.

"I missed you, Sarah."

He wasn't making this any easier.

"Collin...." he just looked at me. "Collin, this isn't working for me anymore," I heard myself saying the words but felt like an outsider watching in horror. His body stiffened.

"What do you mean not working for you?" there was an edge to his voice that I didn't recognize.

"I have been with you for all the wrong reasons, Collin. I've been trying so desperately to make you, and everything about you be Thomas, to fill his place, and fix all the brokenness inside of me. And I can't do it to either of us anymore."

"What? Do you think I didn't know that Sarah!?" he stood up.

"You think I don't realize why you fell in love with me?" His face grimaced with pain.

"I never meant to hurt you!" I choked back tears.

"Collin.... I went to Boston... I found out Thomas killed himself!" my voice was shaking noticeably. I know Thomas asked me in his letter to not tell anyone, but I was desperate for Collin to understand. If only he could understand....

"He killed himself? Why would he do that?" Collin looked at me narrow-eyed.

"He wanted to protect us. He made a bad business deal with some people who would've hurt the boys and me." I felt my throat tighten up. "He thought that if he were gone, he could make it all right again. But he was wrong." I felt a surprise gush of bitterness when I said it.

Collin turned and looked out over the yard, and didn't speak for a moment.

Still looking away, he said, "I am sorry that what he did hurt you. But, it sounds like to me, he did what he felt he had to do. I don't think he would've left you if he had a choice."

Collin still didn't turn around.

"But he did leave...." my words were still hanging in the air, and suddenly I felt a strange sensation of bitterness toward Thomas inside of me. Why didn't he come to me and tell me what was going on? Maybe I could've helped. Why did he abandon me here? I was completely lost in thought when I was snapped back to reality by the sound of Collin's voice.

"Sarah?" He turned and faced me. "Why are you leaving me now? I don't understand. Don't you think Thomas would want you to be happy? I love you more than anyone could ever love a woman, and I would do anything to make you happy." His eyes were pleading.

"Collin, I have not been with you for the right reasons. You can't keep living underneath Thomas' shadow. And I have to get out from underneath his shadow too and make a life for myself somehow."

"Wow, Sarah. That's really great! Make a life for yourself?! Who cares who you hurt in the process, right?"

"But Collin, I can't ever love you the way I loved Thomas."

I regretted the words as soon as they came out of my mouth. And the look on his face was devastating.

I expected him to lash out at me. Instead, he came and sat down next to me. I could see there were tears in his eyes. He rubbed his chin like he was deep in thought. I noticed that he hadn't shaved today. He was so handsome. I felt my resolve start to falter.

"Sarah, you're just upset, and you're not thinking clearly," he looked deep into my eyes and put his hand on my knee. I reacted without thinking and immediately pushed it off.

His face was stunned. He stood up and looked at me with disgust. He turned and walked inside of his house letting the screen door slam behind him.

I had to force myself not to chase him down, but I knew that it wasn't right to stay with him only because of Thomas. And that's exactly what I had done. I wouldn't continue to do wrong.

I slowly walked to my car. I was weeping. But I had done, what I set out to do. I had set things right. I looked at his house and actually hoped for one moment; he would come running out and stop me, and tell me how wrong I was. He did not. I looked at his house one last time, put the car in reverse and drove away.

Chapter 26

I can't say how I made it through the days and nights for the weeks following my breakup with Collin. I knew I had made the right decision, but somehow, he found his way into my thoughts all day long. I ignored the feelings. Pushing him out of my heart and mind. I busied myself with helping Emily plan for the wedding. I went to the gym, walked Ash and worked in the garden. I not only shut Collin out of my life, but I was avoiding Betsey too. I just couldn't face her. I was ashamed of Thomas and what he had done. I couldn't tell her. And I was embarrassed about the situation with Collin, even though she had to have known herself that I was only with him because of Thomas. She would not have judged me, but I couldn't handle it right now. Talking about it. Hashing it over. I just wanted to ignore it and make it all go away. Valentine's Day came and went, and I didn't hear from Collin. I was numb and confused. But determined to build a life for myself. I deserved that much.

Emily wanted to do an 1800's theme wedding and was looking for some old doors to use as props. We had scoured every single antique and thrift shop in and around Wilmington and hadn't been able to find the right style doors. I suggested to her that we try some Antique shops around Raleigh. It was Monday morning, and I logged onto my computer and did a search for Antique Shops. Hoping to find some that we had overlooked. When I put in my search terms, Then Again Antiques in Selma, popped up as one of the first suggestions. I was stunned for a moment. I couldn't believe I had forgotten about that place. I called and told Emily about the store, but she was too busy with school to make the drive out there. So, I decided to go alone. I knew exactly what she was looking for and I could call her if I had a question.

The drive passed pretty quickly, and soon I was sitting outside of the place where I had driven to just months ago after I met Collin. A pang of sadness hit me, and I pushed it away.

I walked inside, and the wood floor creaked as I walked across. It still smelled of old paper and slightly musty. A young girl was working behind the counter; she barely acknowledged me, she was too busy staring at her smartphone. I wondered what happened to the lady who had been so kind to me that day. That fateful day. The day I met Thomas.

I couldn't help but look over at the spot where I had nearly fainted. The place where Thomas walked up to me and introduced himself. Without even realizing it, I walked over to the spot. And I slid down the wall and sat on the floor. The same place I had sat almost 25 years ago. I thought about how much I had changed since that day. How naïve and young I had been. Where had the time gone? Where had I gone? The girl I once was, long gone now. I *had* seen glimpses of her again when I was with Collin, but now just a shell of her existed.

The girl looked over at me curiously.

"Ma'am, are you okay?"

"Oh, I'm fine, just taking a break," I replied.

That seemed to appease her, and she went back to staring at her phone.

I sat looking at the things around me. Everything was different, yet it was all the same. Lost and forgotten items from the past. The only thing that hadn't changed was that the old trunk was still there. I couldn't believe that no one had bought it in all those years. I felt as forgotten as that old trunk.

The front door opened and two young boys walked in. My mind blurred. And for a moment, all I could see was Thomas and his friend, who had walked in the same way. It was like time was repeating itself. I stood up and rushed toward them, and I was just about to call out Thomas' name when the two boys looked over at me. Suddenly reality set in and I could see them clearly. It was not Thomas, and I was not the young Sarah I once was. They were staring at me, a little startled.

My face burned with embarrassment. I ran out of the store and got into my car. The tears began to pour out.

"How could you Thomas? How could you leave me like this?" I hit the steering wheel. I was sobbing now, and I couldn't stop. I was so angry. Angry at me, angry at Thomas, angry at Collin for making me feel what it was like to love again. Things were easier when I was dead right along with Thomas. Now I have to feel all of this.

My phone started to ring. I looked at it. It was Betsey. I don't know why I answered, but I did.

She immediately knew I was crying.

"Oh my god, Sarah what's wrong?"

"I am a big mess, Betsey!" The words were jumbled up with my sobs.

"Oh honey, where are you? I'm coming..." Betsey was clearly worried.

"I'm in Selma...," I said while blowing my nose and trying to balance the phone.

"Selma!? What are you doing in Selma!?" she sounded genuinely alarmed.

"I don't know..." I trailed off.

"Well, come back right now, and come straight to my house. Can you drive?"

"Yes, okay... I'll be there in a bit," There was no use in resisting. I knew Betsey well enough that she wasn't going to take no for an answer.

We hung up, and I got a napkin out of the glove box and blew my nose again. The two boys from the store walked by my car, and they were staring at me. I looked down and pretended I couldn't see them.

The drive back passed more slowly. My thoughts were tormenting me. I pulled into Betsey's driveway, and she ran out to meet me. When I got out of the car, she hugged me tightly.

"Come inside, and I will make you some tea."

We went inside and sat down in her euro style living room. All her furniture came from Sweden. I always loved the simple Scandinavian design that she used.

I sat down on her couch. She brought a glass of iced tea for each of us and sat on the chair opposing me.

I sipped my tea, not making eye contact. I could feel my eyes and face were swollen from crying.

"What is going on, Sarah?" Betsey peered intently at me.

I told her the whole story about Thomas' laptop, Neil's words, the letter from Thomas, the note in the kindred spirit box, seeing my parents, breaking it off with Collin.

Her eyes filled up with tears. She came and sat down next to me on the couch and hugged me again.

"I'm so sorry...."

I just shrugged.

"I am going to tell you something though, Sarah. You may not like what I have to say, but it needs to be said. You need to forgive Thomas for what he did. What he did, he did out of love. I wish like hell it didn't happen, but we can't change the past. Thomas is gone. He has been gone for a long time. But honestly, more than anything, you need to forgive yourself. You have blamed yourself for Thomas' death from day one. If only you had gotten up and gone with him that morning. Right? Thomas knew you wouldn't go that morning. It is not your fault. Thomas knew you wouldn't get up! He planned it that way. He knew what he was doing. Thomas was a planner, and I know that he planned this out completely. You have to let go of the guilt! You never even fully grieved because you were too busy feeling guilty. You haven't allowed yourself to live a real life because of it. For some reason, God or the Universe, whatever you want to call it, saw fit to send you that dream and that note instructing you to let go. But I really think it was not to let go of Thomas, as much as it was to let go of the guilt you're carrying around. Thomas gave his all to you, Sarah. That was Thomas. He loved you more than life itself. That's why it was a simple decision for him to protect you and the boys. It's awful and it's heartbreaking, but it is time to move on. Thomas' death should not be your life's theme."

I looked at her, and she grabbed my hand and squeezed.

I began to realize that she was exactly right. I had spent the last, almost 15 years now, keeping his death alive. I had thrived on him being gone. And simmered in my own guilt. It was what kept me going. I didn't even realize it until now.

"That's why you broke it off with Collin. You didn't think you were worthy of love again. But seeing you with Collin reminded me of the old Sarah. The Sarah who was so full of life and joy. You and Collin belong together, Sarah. You need to make it right between you and him."

"But I can't, Betsey! I was with him for the wrong reasons. I was only with him because he reminded me of Thomas. And that was wrong of me!"

Betsey laughed, "Sarah, what you loved about Collin was Collin. You are not giving yourself enough credit."

I thought of Collin's warm laugh and how safe I felt when I was with him. Maybe she was right. But I didn't know if I could let go of my doubts and fears.

"I am afraid of loving him, Betsey; I don't want to be hurt again."

"I know. Love is a scary thing. It is the most powerful force in this world. It can heal us, or it can destroy us. But love cannot be denied. You can run from it, but running won't protect you from being hurt again. And love will not just go away. Not real love, not the kind of love you have with Collin." She spoke with deep compassion.

I didn't know what to say. I knew she was right. All these weeks I had been away from Collin hadn't changed how I felt about him. I was just pretending I didn't need him when I did.

"He's probably moved on by now, Betsey; it's been weeks," I trailed off.

"That's a chance worth taking, in my opinion." She smiled gently.

***

I got home around 2 pm. Put Ash's leash on and took him for a walk. It was a beautiful Spring afternoon. People were out on their porches and children were playing in the yards. I walked along the sidewalk and thought about what Betsey had said.

Being with Collin had brought me to life. I thought it was only because of Thomas, but a ghost can't really make you feel alive again. Collin made me feel alive again. I missed him. I wanted him. Not because of Thomas. In fact, in all those months together, of comparing him to Thomas, I never wished he was different. I loved him just as he was. My heart suddenly leaped for joy. I loved him just as he was! I loved Collin for Collin, just like Betsey said. I knew I would always love Thomas, but I was free to love Collin. To give myself to him!

I practically ran home. My mind raced. Where would he be right now? I needed to find him. I called his cell phone, and it was off. I tried his office, and the voicemail said the office was closed on Mondays.

I would chance it and go to his house. I picked up Ash and put him in the car, and we drove to Belville.

As I drove down the gravel drive, my heart was racing. I didn't know what to expect when I pulled up. He might not be there. He could be there with another woman. He may not even want to see me. But I had to try.

I walked up on the porch and rang the bell. He didn't answer. Ash laid down, stretched out, and made himself at home.

I opened the screen door and knocked on the paned glass in the door. Still no answer. I closed the screen door and walked around the back of the house. And once I got in view of the river, I could see him. He was down on the dock.

I walked across the yard. My stomach was in knots.

I walked quietly down the dock. He was standing at the end winding up some rope. His back was to me, and he was whistling.

"Collin?"

He turned and looked at me.

For a moment, time stood still. His face had absolutely no reaction. Then suddenly, a smile spread across his face.

"It's about time!"

I ran to him, and he wrapped me up in his arms. His mouth was warm and sweet on mine.

I buried my head in shoulder

"I'm so sorry..."

He gently pushed me back so he could look into my eyes. Tears were streaming down my face.

"Shhh, it's okay now. All that matters is that you are here with me now."

He kissed the tears on my face.

Suddenly, there were tiny footsteps on the dock. Ash came running down toward us.

"Hi, there fella!" Collin bent down and tousled Ash's furry head.

He grabbed my hand, and we walked together, the three of us, back to the house.

***

The first rays of sunlight peeked through the drapes, and I rolled over and felt for Collin in the dim light. Please be there. He was, and still naked. That was a first. My skin warmed at the thought of his body on mine. We made love maybe four times last night. I had lost count. Then we had fallen asleep in each other's arms. It just felt so right to be with him. Nothing was hanging over us anymore. I was free. He stirred and then stretched. He turned to look at me and saw me looking at him. He reached over and touched my face and softly whispered my name.

"Sarah."

I grabbed his hand and pulled it to my lips, kissing it.

He slowly crawled out of bed. He pulled back the covers and sat on the edge of the bed with his back to me and suddenly as I was looking at him, I saw something familiar. In the faint light of morning, I strained to look. Yes, I could see something for sure. My heart pounded loudly. There was a centipede scar, there on his left buttock. How had I not seen it before!? I realized that I had never seen him fully naked. I reached out in disbelief and put my hand on it. "Thomas?!" He turned back around and smiled softly. Then he put his finger to his lips. "Shhhhh! You have to remember, it's Collin now...."

He came around to my side of the bed, and he kissed me. Long and sweet. As he was looking into my eyes and a tear rolled down his cheek. I reached up and wiped it away. He looked lovingly at me with those blue eyes that can see right through you and I know. I finally understand all he did and why. I think of his sticky note, to protect his family at all costs. And that's exactly what he did. He gave up his own life to save us. But somehow, here he was with me again. He had found a way to recreate himself. And he came back to me. Our love had endured. Our love had defied the laws of death and time. I smiled because I knew all along. In my heart, I knew. My Thomas had come back to me. He smiled back at me and got up to go shower. He gave me another kiss before walking away. And I rolled over and sighed, tasting that sweet familiar taste on my lips with his smell all around me. I fell back asleep with his name on my breath.

Epilogue

2002

I never expected to be saved. I never expected the fishermen who faces were worn like soft leather and spoke not a word of English, to haul me from the sea with the last breath of life in my lungs. As my limp body laid upon the cracked wooden deck of their boat, I looked up at the sky. I thought of my beautiful Sarah, and I wept in defeat. I had failed her...again.

The circumstances leading up to this moment were surreal. Almost like scenes out of a B run movie.

Bad investments. Check.

Loan sharks. Check.

Failed attempts to raise money to pay them back. Check.

Them coming to collect. Check.

I had foolishly gone to Vinnie Francini, a known local mobster for help. It was supposed to be a temporary loan. Only a few weeks, I told him. I just wanted to make good on my promises to my clients. They trusted me when I made promises about a big payout from investing in a company called Stefanburg Paper Inc. It was a small paper company that was being bought out by a larger corporation. The word was that the stock was going to quadruple after the merger. What I didn't know, was that George Stefanburg was one step away from bankruptcy, and the deal fell through 1 hour before the papers were signed. His company's stock was worth pennies before the day closed. I sat looking at the ticker tape on the television set and tried to scramble for an idea. Any idea. I couldn't take delivering the devastating news to my clients, that I lost most, if not all, of their savings. If I just had some seed money, I could turn this around before anyone really noticed. And that idea is how I ended up borrowing the money from Vinnie. I took the loan money and made some new investments that paid off a little, but not the amount that I needed. I was going to have to take risks that I would usually never take. I felt confident that all would be okay. I had a knack for making money in the market, a natural instinct. Over the next couple of weeks, I made numerous investments, and all of them failed. I even took money from our personal IRA and savings to float some more investments. Everything was a bust. I had somehow lost my "magic touch" and all my practical sense of reasoning. The calls were starting to come in as clients were getting their monthly statements in the mail. It was getting ugly, and there was nothing I could do. And to make matters worse, Vinnie was sending his men over to give me a "past due" message. I could take them beating me up, threatening me, and even tearing up my office. But when they threatened my family, all bets were off. I had to do something and do something quickly.

I did the last thing I ever wanted to do. I sucked up my pride and went to see Sarah's Dad. I sat in my car at the entrance gate wanting nothing more, than to turn around and leave. But I was not afforded the choice. The gates opened and I drove up the driveway. Edmund met me at the door. And Marie soon followed. Both hugged me and asked a million questions about Sarah and the boys. Edmund and Marie felt more like family than Sarah's parents ever did. Sarah rarely wanted to come here, so it had been a while since they had seen them. I got out my wallet and showed them the boy's recent school photos. Edmund then took me into the drawing room, and Marie brought in some tea. They made a little more small talk, but soon they were off to take care of their duties. I sat on the couch and looked around at the grandness of the room. I couldn't believe that Sarah gave all of this up, to be with me. And look at me now. A complete failure. Here to beg help from her father.

I was lost in thought when I heard Mr. Cargill enter the room.

I stood up and went to shake his hand. He shook my hand, but reluctantly.

My heart was pounding. The man was so intimidating, but I could not let my feelings show. He was the kind of man who could sense weakness a mile away.

"Mr. Cargill, I appreciate you taking the time to see me."

His eyes were devoid of emotion.

"Well, get on with it." He demanded.

"I need your help, sir. I have unfortunately made some bad investments recently, and lost my clients quite a bit of money. I was hoping that if I could borrow some money from you, that I could make this right." I tried not to let my voice betray me.

"Why in the world would I help you?" he scoffed. "I have no interest in bailing you out."

My heart sank. I knew that I would have to tell him the whole story.

"That's not just it." I looked down at the floor.

"I borrowed some money from a loan shark to re-invest, and I failed again. Now they are out for blood. My blood. Because I can't pay them back."

He started to laugh, a deep sinister laugh.

"What gave you the idea that I would be interested in helping you out of your mess?"

I felt the shame rising up from my gut, but I continued. I was desperate. My heart was pounding so loudly; I could barely hear myself speaking.

"I just need to pay them back; and maybe with a little extra, I can begin to fix this mess that I made. I have a high rate of success in my investments usually. This has never happened to me before. There was a paper company that...." He didn't let me finish. "Honestly, I don't care how or why you are in this situation. You are wasting my time, and I would like for you to leave now."

I felt a sob rise up in my throat.

"They are threatening Sarah and the children now, and if I don't pay them back soon, they're going to kill me."

"Is that so?" he laughed again, almost under his breath.

"I wish I could say I was sorry to hear that. You have been an embarrassment to this family since the day you showed up. Sarah's biggest mistake in life was marrying you. You ruined her life. And you are going to have to get yourself out of this mess. I have no interest in helping you."

He started to walk out of the room but turned back around.

"On the bright side, now Sarah will see what kind of man you really are." And he smiled a satisfied smile, and then he disappeared out of sight. I stood there paralyzed. I never expected him to say no. I knew he would make it hard for me, but I never thought he would actually say no! It took everything I had inside of me to come to him like this! The humiliation was unbearable. And he said no! He didn't even care about Sarah and the boys. I was enraged; but more than that, I was terrified. I was entirely out of options.

223

That was the night I realized I was worth more dead than I was alive. I was sitting at my desk, and I was going through some documents and came across my life insurance statement. I grimly realized that I had the answer. But some plans would have to be made, and it would not be easy. I upped the policy to cover all of the debt to Vinnie, put the money I had lost back into my client's accounts, and to set Sarah up for life. I went home and talked Sarah into buying a house in Wilmington, North Carolina. We had been talking about moving there "one day," and I would just rush the process along. I knew that once I was gone, she would not stay here in Massachusetts. She would need a place to go.

I knew I had to kill myself without the insurance agency finding out that it was a suicide or Sarah wouldn't get a dime. I researched and was coming up with dead ends. Then I remembered an article I had read a few weeks earlier, about the dangers of rip currents, and gloomily decided that drowning would be my path.

I had been promising Sarah that I would take her to Mexico, so I bought our tickets for the next week. I surprised her with the trip, and she was so excited. Inside I was cringing because only I knew the truth of why we were going. It would be wonderful though, to spend my last days with her. Just the two of us. Something that would give me the strength to do what I had to do.

I researched all I could about the ocean currents, and about how the insurance company would handle a drowning death. I wanted to make sure all my bases were covered. Then, I wrote Sarah a goodbye letter. I needed her to hear an explanation from me. There was no talking to her about it beforehand. And I could not just leave her without a goodbye. She was my everything. She and the boys were all that mattered to me. And I would protect them at all costs. Just when my determination was starting to falter, I was given a very clear message from Vinnie, that the debt wasn't the only thing I owed him now. He was pissed, and I was dead either way. I was going down this path, like it or not.

I talked to Neil, trying to prep him without actually telling him my plan. But, he was so distraught over the whole situation. I could barely get anything explained to him. Neil was an emotional kind of guy. He had been such a great friend to me. I hated to see him so upset. So, I didn't say much more. I wrote down a plan of action and left it on his desk. When he came into my office and asked me about it, I told him it was a provisional, just in case anything happened to me. Knowing all along, that he would think it was about Vinnie and his men. I also gave him a key to safety deposit box, where I left the letter to Sarah. I knew that one day, she would come to him with questions, and he could give her the key then. By then the insurance company's investigation would be long over. I didn't want anything to go wrong.

It was a beautiful morning, and I had just spent the last five days in paradise with my beautiful wife. I walked out to the cabana and sat on the sandy beach. The sun was just starting to come into view. The color was spectacular. My heart was gripped with pain at the thought of dying, but I had no choice. If I loved Sarah, if I truly loved her, then this is what I would have to do. I had every intention to die. You would have thought I would have been afraid of dying, yet somehow, I wasn't. I was firm in my decision. Doing what I had to do. This was my responsibility to bear, mine and mine alone. Everything was in place as I walked out into the water, I looked back one more time at the cabana, where Sarah was sleeping, and I whispered one last "I love you." The water was warm as I moved forward and swam out into the deeper part of the ocean. I kept swimming out, further and further, waiting for the current to take me. Somehow, with all my meticulous plans, the universe had something else in mind for me that day.

We were on that small fishing vessel for what seemed like several hours while I vomited up sea water and drifted in and out of consciousness. I had no idea where we were. I didn't know how long or how far I had drifted with the currents. I could smell fish and sea air. Occasionally, I was splashed by a wave that came over the deck. I could hear the men talking, but I couldn't understand them. We finally arrived at a small village where the men lived. They took me immediately to a ramshackle old building, which I later learned was their hospital. It was primitive at best, with a straw-covered roof and paper-thin walls. A man in a white coat and a stethoscope around his neck examined me and spoke in Spanish to me, hoping for some recognition. My high school and college Spanish had long left me, and I had no idea what he was saying, except for the occasional "Sì, senòr." I was in shock and completely exhausted from the ordeal. I laid there while they cared for me and asked nothing in return. I developed a significant cough within a day and a high fever. I was delirious the first few days. Waking and sleeping intermittently. I was fed pills, which I assumed were antibiotics. Soon the fever subsided, but I was still very weak. As I began to recover, I waited for the police to come and question me. Or for a search party to come and find me here. There was a small tv in a room adjacent from me. I could hear it playing all day and night. I assumed my face would be plastered on it.

Yet no one came for me, and my name was never mentioned on the television. I was completely baffled. I would lie there lost in my thoughts and memories. I'd close my eyes and see the boys playing, and I'd see my Sarah smiling at me. God, she was beautiful. And the tears would flow down my cheeks. I missed them so much. I contemplated what I should do. I could go back and risk all I had sacrificed and hoped that somehow, I could find another way out of the mess I had created. But I knew, there was no other path. I had tried everything. Then I realized I could stay dead. Thomas Avery had died that day after all. No one knew me. No one was looking for me. I had gotten my wish. Sarah would collect the life insurance, and pay those men back. And she would be safe. That's all I ever wanted was for her and the boys to be safe. I had put them in danger, and I had to fix it. My life in exchange for theirs. Sounded like a fair deal to me. As I recovered, my mind twisted and turned, not wanting to be away from them by choice. All I had to do was pick up the phone.

One phone call and I would be with my family again. In desperation once, I picked up a phone at the nurse's desk and tried to dial Sarah. I thought of her sweet voice on the other end and how happy she'd be to hear from me, and I hung up. She wasn't the only one who'd be interested in my resurrection. The loan sharks and the insurance company would be all too happy to hear from me. So, I'd either be dead by their hands or at best, be imprisoned. They would never think that my survival was accidental. They would think I planned it this way. And in the end, Sarah would still be hurt. I wouldn't do that to her. I couldn't.

After a few weeks, I was fully recovered. I was provided a shirt and pair of pants and escorted to the door. The nurse handed me a piece of paper that I could not read, and then she hugged me. They had done nothing but show me kindness. I was sad to leave. I walked out of there a man with no money, no name, and no home.

I walked along an empty dirt road in the scorching heat. I had no idea of where I was and no idea of what to do. I was going to need another miracle.

That miracle came in the shape of an old Chevrolet pickup truck. A faded red 1960's model with rust all over it. It was driven by an older lady named Consuela. She spoke a little English, she pulled over and asked me if I needed a ride.

I went home with her, and she fed me a nice meal of fresh corn tortillas and black beans, with a beer. Better than any Mexican food Sarah and I had ever eaten. She asked if I was in need of work and offered me a job in exchange for room and board. She was an indigenous farmer, and I helped her with her crops of maize, beans, peppers, and fruit. It was hard work, but I was happy to be busy.

She didn't ask my name until the next day. I said, Collin Young. Why Collin Young? I had no idea; it was just the first thing that popped into my head. So that's the name that stuck. Thomas was dead, and I was reborn as Collin.

I tried to keep my mind off of Sarah and the boys by working every day as hard as I possibly could. I spent a lot of time with Consuela. She was like a mother to me. She would always say "Usted trabaja demasiado duro" which was Spanish for "you work too hard." My Spanish improved remarkably. I learned more from Consuela in 3 months, than I had in my three years of Spanish in high school. She never pressed me about my history. She just accepted me as I was. And I was incredibly grateful for that.

After six months of working for Consuela, her son came to visit. He was visiting from America and spoke fluent English. He was a tall guy with jet black hair. His name was Felipe. He was super friendly to me right from the start. We became good friends. He came to visit his mom regularly, and we would hang out each time he came. He was in school at San Diego State University in California, on an exchange student program. And he had just recently secured a work visa for after graduation. When he would come for a visit, we would go to the local bar and drink beer. The beautiful senoritas were always glad to see us come in. They would come over to the table and talk to us. Batting their eyelashes and leaning over the table to give us a good look at their cleavage. Felipe would sometimes go home with one, but not me; I could not bear the thought of being with another woman. I was Sarah's, even in death.

That's how I lived for three years. One day after another, working hard and trying not let myself think or remember. Being isolated from the real world was a benefit. I kept my mind on my work, and that helped to numb the pain. Then one day, Consuela became very ill without warning. She died before the town doctor even arrived. I sat by her bedside and cried. I was devastated. I loved Consuela, and she was the only home I had in this world. When Felipe came to bury his mother, he insisted I come back to America with him. I was very hesitant, but I figured California was far enough away from my past to keep me isolated. The biggest issue I was facing, was not having any documentation. When I told Felipe, he asked no questions, only stated, "I know a guy who can help." Before long, I had a social security number, a birth certificate, and a California Driver's license, all with the name Collin Young. It was official.

I lived with Felipe in San Francisco. He had moved there after College to work. I got a job and worked as a handyman for the apartment complex. It was an easy job and let me acclimate slowly back to living in America. But after a year, I decided I wanted to do more with my life. I thought real estate was the best path to get me back on my feet, so I signed up for classes, and within six months I was a licensed realtor.

Selling real estate came naturally to me. I was always good with people, and selling houses flowed naturally into my gifting. It wasn't long before I was able to move out on my own. When I moved into a small house down in Excelsior, I finally realized how alone I really was. Being with Consuela and then Felipe had kept me busy enough to ignore the pain inside of me but now I had no choice but to face those feelings. I wondered about Sarah and the boys. It had been five years since I last saw their faces. I didn't even have a photo. My wallet was lost in the ocean when I was pulled under.

I wandered the streets. Looking at the faces of people passing by. Loneliness consumed me.

I wanted to go back to Sarah. I wanted to hold her in my arms and tell her how much I still loved her. But doing so would put us both in grave danger. Five years was not long enough for anyone to forget, especially people like Vinnie Francini. So, I pushed the thoughts of returning from my mind. But never Sarah, she lived there in my daily thoughts. I dreamed of her night and day. Praying for a way, one day, to be with her again.

After nine years of selling real estate, I had become a great success. I was the top realtor in the area. Money was rolling in. I kept living in my modest home, saving every penny that I made. I had a few friends. I was good at being Collin Young. I was starting to forget what it was like to be Thomas. I had changed so much, that I was really a new person. I splurged and bought a brand-new BMW Sedan Series 3. Something Thomas would have never done. But having a nice car impressed clients and it sure was a pleasure to drive. I had even gone on a few dates but I never enjoyed them, I was flat emotionally. Most of the time, the girl would end up leaving early. And I didn't care. Sarah's face haunted my every moment. No one could replace her.

I volunteered to represent my office at the career fair at Berkley University. No one else wanted to go, and since I had no appointments lined up for that day, I figured I would go. I set up my booth and took a seat at the table. The students rolled in unenthusiastically. A few stopped by my booth and asked questions about how much money I made a month. No one really cared that I was there. They had their eyes on bigger game. A young guy came up to my booth and smiled at me. He said he was waiting for his girlfriend who was at the Belle Fashion Industries Booth right now. We both laughed. Something was striking about this kid. Something so familiar, yet I was sure that I had never seen him before. He had sandy blonde hair and blue eyes. I kept looking at his face; he was so familiar. In fact, so familiar that I started to wonder. Then I did the math, Blake and Adam were both college age now. But it couldn't be.... could it!? I kept him there by making small talk. He told me he was majoring in business, just like his dad. I asked him what his dad did for a living. He paused for a moment and said: "My dad died." My heart jumped in my chest. I tried to act nonchalant. This was probably just a sheer coincidence, but I couldn't ignore it. Just then his girlfriend, a pretty girl with long dark curly hair, came up and said: "I'm hungry, let's go get some food."

He turned and looked at me. "Nice talking to you!"

I was panicking. I didn't want him to leave.

I called out as he was walking away, "I didn't get your name..."

"Blake Avery," he smiled, and they disappeared into the crowd.

It took everything I had inside of me not to run after him. I wanted to hug him. I wanted to know all about his life. But he wouldn't know me anyway. And after all, his father had died.

After that moment I was consumed, thinking about Blake, Adam, and of course, my Sarah.

I looked for Blake everywhere I went, but in a city of 850,000 people, the chances were slim to none I would run into him again.

I beat myself up for not asking more questions. How would I ever find him again? All my chances of finding out about Sarah were gone. At least I knew he was happy and had a good life. But I couldn't stop thinking about him. Thinking about Sarah and

Adam. Wanting to see them too. But what did it matter anyway? Thomas was dead. That was it! Thomas was dead, but I wasn't! Maybe, if Sarah fell in love with me once, she would fall in love with the new me too. I had to know; it was a chance worth taking. I had some guilt about intruding into her life after all this time, but I ignored it. Sarah was my love. She was my everything, and I was completely lost without her. I had to find her.

I searched google looking for her name. Nothing pulled up. I tried to find Adam and Blake, as well. Their Social Media pages pulled up but revealed no information about where they lived. I couldn't friend them and keep my plan. When I saw Adam's profile picture, I recognized him immediately. He had the same face as he did when he was 8. My heart ached. I felt so sad about all the years I missed. My boys were men now.

I finally decided to hire a private investigator to find Sarah for me. I hired the best guy in the city. His name was Stanley Berkowitz. He was happy to take the case but did give me the side eye when I wouldn't tell him why I was looking for her. I gave him a fake name and a throwaway phone number. If I was going to pull this off, I couldn't be traced back to this guy.

The next day he called me and told me he had found her. And most importantly, she was still single. She had never remarried and was living in Wilmington, just as I had predicted. I asked Stanley to fly out there and watch her for me. I wanted a report of her habits and routines. That way I could plan how she would meet me. If she could just love me for who I am now, then I know I could trust her with the truth. Maybe then, she won't see me as a failure.

After two weeks, he came back, and his report was in my hands, Sarah lived a pretty predictable life. She was making this all too easy for me. I quit my job and moved to Wilmington. I bought a house in Bellville. A house I knew Sarah would love. A big white house with a huge front porch, situated right on the river. I paid cash and moved in right away. It was everything I could do to not immediately try to find Sarah, but I knew patience was the key to success. I quickly got a job at a local real estate office. It was great to be in the South again.

Stanley told me that Sarah had weekly lunch dates with her friend Betsey. I was so happy to know that Betsey had moved here to be with Sarah. I am sure that was a big help to Sarah.

I decided that I would "run" into her on the street after one of those lunch dates. I hoped there was still something about me that she would find attractive. I had a little concern that she would recognize me, but my hair was so much lighter now, it lightened and greyed as I got older. My face was definitely showing its age too. I believed that there was enough difference now, that I could pass for someone else. 14 years makes a big difference in your appearance, or so I thought.

The day I decided to have my run in with her, I was a nervous wreck. I felt like an awkward kid. I was so anxious, I went ahead downtown early, even though I planned to "meet" her after her lunch. I drank coffee at Lila's Bistro, and then went to People's Bank to deposit a check. I got caught up in the middle of a crowd that had gathered outside of the bank because there had been an attempted bank robbery earlier that morning. I wasn't thinking about the fact that Sarah would be coming down the street any minute to meet Betsey. I stepped out of the crowd, and suddenly, there she was. And still just as beautiful as ever. My Sarah. Time stopped for just a moment. 14 years had passed, and nothing had changed. I loved her just as much as I did the day I last saw her. She was headed straight in my direction. I wasn't sure what to do, but it was too late. Her eyes had met mine. The moment she saw me, her face went pale, and she fell to the ground. Instinctively, I ran to her side. As she opened her eyes and looked at me, I had to resist the overwhelming urge to kiss her right then and there. But I couldn't, I wasn't Thomas anymore, I was Collin, a complete stranger.

Instead, I offered. "Ma'am, are you okay? Can you hear me, Ma'am?"

The Dark Room

A dark and steamy thriller that will keep you on the edge of your seat.

Straight-laced Anna finds herself in a steamy extramarital affair with a noir film photographer Alec Prentice. He's sexy and irresistible, drawing her into his world of sex and seduction. But soon his bad boy ways, and her guilty conscious consumes her and pushes her to end the affair abruptly. Not long after ending the affair, she frighteningly realizes she is being stalked. As she continues her attempt to keep the affair a secret, the stalking escalates. Even when it begins to jeopardize her safety, she refuses to get help for fear of her secret being exposed. Forcing her to take matters into her own hands and leads her down a path of deception and violence. As a hurricane bears down on the coastal city of Wilmington North Carolina, she finds herself alone with a gun clutched to her chest as she faces her stalker and his terrifying secret. Leaving her fighting for her life and for everything else that ever mattered.

Coming Early 2018

Sign up for the VIP list to be the first to know and receive exclusive discount pricing.

NatalieBanks.net